I0616522

THE INBETWEENS
THE CROSSING

BY NIKKI AKSAMIT

ISBN 978-0615643519
Text copyright © 2012 by Nikki Aksamit
All rights reserved. Published by R3 Publishing, 85226.

For Rook, Rohan and Reesyn – I love you more.

Introduction

The villages that spread across the Middle Lands were separated into four, The North Village, The South Village, The East Village and The West Village. They had little contact with each other, as it was a time before roads had been made to connect them and there was quite a distance between. Travel during this time was done on foot, as no wild animal had yet been domesticated enough to carry a rider. Only those few who bravely walked the many days and nights to their neighbors, and had made it back safely, could speak of what life was like outside their own village.

There were small groups of rocky foothills scattered here and there across the Middle Lands, some surrounding beautiful crystal clear lakes. The pleasantly mild climate was only interrupted during the first and third seasons, when harsh winds and rains would sweep across the prairies, sometimes leaving great destruction in their path. The villages had been nestled between the rocky hills to protect them from these violent storms.

Daily life in the four villages was simple. Each self sustaining, its residents grew their own fruits, vegetables and grain. They hunted in the dense forests for animal meat, wove their own fabrics and all tools were hand made. Fresh water came from the plentiful rivers and streams that crisscrossed the plains and from wells dug deep into its rich brown soil. The cottages in all of the villages were mostly alike, large domed structures made from the flat stones found on the floors of underground caves and sealed with the sandy dirt found at the base of the foothills.

Councils had been set up to govern the thousands of people in each village, and though there was little theft or deceit

4

during these times, laws and punishments has been put in place to ensure the safety of the citizens. Children attended daily lessons when they were of age, learning about the history and future plans of the councils. They were taught the fundamentals of reasoning, as well as manual skills such as sewing and archery. After the lesson day was complete, the children went home to help with chores, and to look after the younger children while their parents went about the running of the village. The children's free time was spent playing in the fields and swimming in the lakes. The few younger children who dared to would even try to climb the foothills now and again, in spite of their parents warning that this was something best left until they were older.

It was a time of great story telling, and all four of the villages kept written records of the events that had come to pass. When an Adventurer, as they were called in the West Village, ventured out to explore the land outside of their village they returned with drawings of the terrain and accounts of life in the surrounding villages. It was hoped that some day soon bridges could be built, and the land could be leveled where needed, so as to create roads which would allow for the villages to trade goods and supplies.

It was the stories told by the groups of children who were sent on the cross country journey of The Crossing however which were regarded as of the highest importance. It was from these tales that the council learned what was needed to teach all of the children, and from which future leaders were chosen. Every child who set out on The Crossing returned home with a different story to tell, as no journey was ever quite the same. But there were times, thankfully few and far between, when one or more of the children could not tell the story of what had occurred on the path of

5

The Crossing. They could not tell their stories because these were the children who never returned home at all.

Chapter 1

The three children stood in a row at the beginning of the path. A gathering of family, friends and even some who they did not know had come to offer their well wishes, and see them on their way. There was much talk, laughing and singing. It was a warm spring morning, and even the birds seemed to join in the celebration as they chirped merrily from the trees. Most who had gathered in the clearing to see the children off had already made the journey of The Crossing many years ago, and they knew that its path would be different, as it was each time. Only that the path started at the South side of their village and finished at the North side remained the same. The terrain of the path and the directions the journey would take were always changing.

On the left was The Blue. On the right was The Yellow. The Red was in the middle. These were not their real names of course, these were the names given to them for The Crossing. Color names were given to the children by the elders so that their true names could not be heard by those on the path who would use them for trickery. The bright bands that each had on their left arm were also there to help should one of the children get lost during their journey.

The Blue was Brynn. Brynn was twelve years old, and quite tall for her age. Her hair, which hung long and straight to the middle of her back, was the color of a winter sunset, and her eyes were the color of a brand new leaf. Brynn was excited to start The Crossing.

The Yellow was Paulo. At eleven, Paulo was the youngest and quite small for his age. His hair, which was always messy, was the same black as a moonless night and his eyes were the same blue as the sky after the rain. Paulo was dreading The Crossing.

Not too tall, and not too small, The Red was Ryu. At twelve and a half, he was the oldest of the three. The same brown as many other children, Ryu's hair had the habit of flopping down into his eyes as he spoke, eyes that were a different color almost every day, changing to match his mood or to match his feelings at any given moment. Although Ryu was a little anxious, he was also very happy. He had been waiting for The Crossing forever it seemed, and now it was finally time. Because he was the eldest, Ryu was entrusted with the compass by the elders. Only one was given to each group of children who set out on The Crossing, and the compass was the only tool they were given to find their way home. It hung from a long piece of twine around Ryu's neck.

Each wore the identical uniform of The Crossing, a long sleeve tunic of light brown burlap and matching long pants tucked into tall animal skin walking boots. A small cloth pouch was fastened to the long braided rope belt wrapped many times around and tied at their waists. Other than the compass Ryu wore, only the arm band with the color of their given name was different.

Ryu looked at The Blue. Although he had known Brynn and her family all of his life, he forced his mind to think of her now only as The Blue. He knew Brynn well enough to know that she too had been waiting for The Crossing, and she too was pleased that the time had come. Ryu knew she was smart and strong, and that she would do well on The Crossing. He shared a quick smile with her before he turned his eyes toward The Yellow.

8

Ryu did not know The Yellow. He knew his name was Paulo, he had heard his mother speaking to him that morning, but it was easier to think of him as The Yellow than it was to think of Brynn as The Blue.

"The Yellow is very small," thought Ryu as he studied the boy for a moment, "and he is afraid." Ryu felt afraid for him. The Crossing was long, and it was confusing. Many had gotten lost along the path. "I will watch out for him as we go." Ryu told himself. "He will need a friend."

And just as The Yellow looked up to meet Ryu's gaze, The Horn sounded. It was time. They stood there at the beginning, the three of them, staring out at what lay ahead. The Horn blew once more. Ryu stood up tall, preparing himself for the long journey. Brynn was quivering with excitement and anticipation. Tears started to cloud Paulo's bright blue eyes. The Final Horn blew, loud and long, and it was The Blue, Brynn, who took the first step forward. Everyone cheered and clapped.

"Do not hurry!" Brynn's mother called out after her as she watched her daughter rush away from the start.

"He is ready." Ryu's mother said to his father, touching his arm with a smile, her words full of pride.

"He will be fine." Paulo's mother said softly to herself as she wrung her hands together nervously, secretly wishing she could embrace him just one last time.

Chapter 2

"But, why do I have to go?" It was The Yellow who spoke. He had not moved. Even though The Final Horn had blown, and The Blue had started on her way, he had not moved.

"Why do I have to go?" he asked again softly, "Why can I not stay here?"

For many hours he had lay awake in bed at night pondering this same question, but now was the first time he had spoken it out loud. He was the oldest of the children in his family, and the first to face The Crossing. He knew the answer to his question of course, his parents had told him every time they spoke of The Crossing. There were many times at the end of the day, when he and his father had been fishing in The River Fish Pond, that his father would tell stories of his own Crossing.

When the sun was going down just behind the big old oak tree that stood tall by the pond, Paulo and his father would sit and rest against that tree before starting the long walk home. His father would tell him many stories of how he made his way along the path of The Crossing. He would tell him about The Riddles, which were different for each group of children who made the journey. He would tell him about The Nothings, and The Somethings and... His father would always stop short at this part of the story and say "You will see."

Paulo knew there were others of which his father did not wish to speak. His mother was the same, she also would not talk about the others that were not The Nothings or The Somethings. Paulo did not know whether or not the others

11

were bad or good. He was afraid to ask. He knew from all the tales he had heard of The Crossing that The Nothings and The Somethings appeared in different forms, no one could say how or when they would appear. But always, at the end of every story told by the pond, his father would ruffle Paulo's already quite messy hair, smile, and say the exact same thing, "Every child must complete The Crossing, it is Our Way."

Paulo loved that big oak by the pond, its branches reaching out in every direction, like it was trying to touch all the corners of the world. He wished he was there right now. It was a quiet place, a calm place, a happy place. Now, with all the noise and cheers around him, he felt neither calm nor happy. He wanted to turn away, to shout, "I am not ready!", but he knew it was too late.

He looked to his parents, with their smiling faces, clapping proudly. He knew that they thought he was ready. They had told him that he was ready for The Crossing. Often, his mother would say how smart he was, and how well she knew he was going to do on The Crossing. Once, he had told her that she was wrong, that he did not think he would do well. He was smaller than the other boys his age, at least a few inches shorter than the shortest. He had never been particularly strong either. While the other children swung on the rope over the pond, running fast to grab it and pushing off to see who could land the farthest out in the water, Paulo could only watch. He was not strong enough to hold on to the rope long enough.

Sometimes, when Paulo came down to the pond and no one else was there, he would try to swing from the rope. Each time was the same, and he would fall into the dirt instead of the pond. The other children thought he was afraid, afraid to swing high, or even to fall into the water. They never made fun or teased him, but after asking the first few times they no longer asked him to join them.

Paulo was not afraid. As a matter of fact, he loved going high, and was an excellent tree climber. Not one of the other children could climb a tree as fast or go as high up in the branches as Paulo could. He had even climbed near the top of the old oak tree. The other children did not know this of course, Paulo climbed trees when he wanted to be alone, or to watch without being seen.

"You are stronger than you think." His mother had answered when he had told her he would not do well on The Crossing. She had touched his arms where Paulo thought there should be muscle, but he had only skin and bones. "Strength does not come from here." she said, and then placed her hands over his heart, "It comes from here. When you need it, it will be there my son, where it has always been."

He did not understand. The older boys who carried the wood, they were strong. The boys who stacked the stones to make new walls, they were strong. A small boy who could not swing out over the pond was not strong. Paulo wished he felt strong now. He wished his knees were not shaking. He wished his heart was not pounding so fast. He wished he was up high in the tall trees that lined both sides of the path of The Crossing, just watching what was going on down below. He wished he was in the branches of the big oak tree by The River Fish Pond, or even back home, safe in his bed. Paulo wished he was anywhere but here at the beginning of The Crossing.

"It is time to go." It was The Red. Paulo did not know his name, but The Red was one of the boys Paulo had seen carrying wood to The Storing Place. He had seen him laughing with his friends, and playing ball in The Green Field. The Red was much taller than Paulo, with muscular arms and legs. His eyes seemed to smile as they met Paulo's, and there was something very comforting about them.

The Red placed his hand on Paulo's shoulder. "I will walk with you." he said, and motioned toward the path.

Knowing that this boy, The Red, would be with him somehow made Paulo a lot less frightened. Somehow, he knew that as long as he stayed close to The Red, everything would be alright. Maybe, just maybe, The Crossing would be easier if he walked beside The Red.

Paulo took a deep breath. With a final glance back to his parents he took his first step away from all that he knew, the first step toward that which he did not know. He took the first step onto the long, winding path. Looking down at the reddish brown dirt, his heart heavy with sadness, Paulo took his first steps on the path of The Crossing.

Chapter 3

Brynn reminded herself not to hurry. Her mother had reminded her of it over and over again in the weeks before The Crossing. "Brynn," she would say, "you must not rush, The Crossing is not a race. There is no prize for finishing first."

Brynn was not one to take her time however, nor did she like to finish anything last. Everything she did, Brynn did very quickly, and with purpose. And even though she had been told time and time again that The Crossing was not a contest, she was unconvinced that there would be no reward if she did in fact finish first. But minding her mother's warning, she slowed her steps, but only slightly. The narrow path was clear, only a stray tree root or small rock jutted out here and there. Brynn could see where the path turned into the trees up ahead, and she felt certain the first Riddle must be just around that corner.

"Each Riddle means something different to the one who reads it." Brynn's mother had told her. "You can not ask another to read it for you. It is a message is for you, and only you."

Brynn was excited about The Riddles. She knew they were of great importance, and that they gave those who were on The Crossing answers that helped them continue on the path. They were like the puzzles her father had given her to do in her lesson book before he passed on to The Great Forever. She smiled at the thought of her father. It had been eight seasons, and the sadness only came sometimes now. Her father had been a teacher to the children, and he had loved to give her problems and puzzles to occupy her mind on those days when the rains were so heavy they kept everyone indoors.

"You have a quick, sharp mind Brynn." He would tell her. *"It will serve you well when your time of The Crossing comes."*

Brynn looked behind her. The Red and The Yellow were still quite far back. Although she did not usually find herself interested in the goings-on of others, Brynn watched them for a moment as she walked. Ryu, "No, you mean The Red!" she scolded herself, was walking with The Yellow. Brynn could not understand why The Red would want to stay with the younger boy. He would be faster and could navigate the narrow path far easier on his own.

Turning to look ahead Brynn did not see a tree root, far larger than the others that had been on the path, until it was too late. Her foot got caught under the thick wood, and over she went. She landed quite hard, but had thought quickly enough to put her hands out in front of her. She pushed herself up to her knees, and sat back on her feet. As she dusted off the dirt, the scrapes on her hands looked awful and stung quite a bit, but there was no blood.

"Silly girl!" she told herself, "This shows why you must always stay focused on where you are going and not worry about what others are doing!" She was angry with herself for being distracted, something she rarely, if ever, let happen now.

She remembered the one time her best friend Lyric had whispered a joke to her while her father's back had been turned during lessons.

"It will serve you well to study hard," her father had been teaching that day, "and to stay focused on the task at hand."

Both girls had laughed out loud at the joke, and her father had sent them outside to The Quiet Time Place. When he joined them a few minutes later, he had told Lyric that her punishment was that she was not to speak even one word in class for the remainder of the week. Lyric had tears in her eyes when Brynn's father had sent her back to the lesson room.

Turning to Brynn, he looked both sad and frustrated at the same time. "If Lyric told you to jump in a poisonous briar bush, would you?" he asked her.

"Pardon me Father?" Brynn had asked, confused.

"It is a simple question, Brynn. If Lyric told you to jump in a poisonous briar bush, would you?"

"Of course not Father," Brynn answered, "that would be foolish." Her father's face softened, and he took her hand in his.

"Is it any less foolish then for Lyric to break The Rules, and for you to decide to do the same? You can not decide for Lyric what she will do, but you, my child, can always decide what to do for yourself."

"Are you alright?" It was The Red.

The boys had seen Brynn fall, and in the moments she was remembering, they had run as fast as they could to come and help her.

"I am fine." Brynn answered, but found she could not meet Ryu's eyes. He offered his hand to help her stand, and only because it was him, did she accept it.

Ryu's father and her father had been friends since childhood. Their families had celebrated holidays and birthdays together. It was Ryu's family who came to stay with her and her mother the day her father passed on. She had many happy memories, as well as sad ones, with Ryu and his family in them. They were friends. Although they had shared many things in the past, as Ryu helped her get to her feet, Brynn knew that The Crossing was something she must do alone.

"Thank you," she said quietly, "but I must be on my way." She turned to continue up the path.

"Can we walk together?" Ryu asked, putting his hand on her arm. He gave her a gentle smile. "It will be much safer with three sets of eyes looking for hazards on the path." And as though it was decided, he nodded his head and said, "We will walk with you."

The heat rose through Brynn instantly. Who was Ryu to decide what she would do? In the years since her father's passing, Brynn had learned to rely on only herself. Her mother had taken the loss very hard, and still cried quietly in her room most of the time. It was left to Brynn to keep things running smoothly. She kept the cottage clean, made most of the meals, washed the laundry and stayed focused on her studies. There was little time left for playing or friends, but it was a routine that Brynn had become accustomed to.

She wanted to tell Ryu that just because he was older, it did not give him the right to decide what she would or would not do. She wanted to tell him that she was just as smart, just as strong as he was. She wanted to tell him that she did not need him to help her, and that she would be fine on her own. But Brynn had always been taught never to speak out in anger, so instead she gently removed his hand and said quite firmly,

"Thank you for your offer The Red, but I would like to carry on by myself." And with a quick turn, she set off toward the bend in the path at a brisk pace, eager to continue The Crossing.

Chapter 4

Moments later, Paulo was still staring after Brynn, but something in the dirt had caught Ryu's eye. Bending down, although it was mostly covered with dirt, he could see that the object was quite shiny. Using his fingers, Ryu dug it out and lifted it from the earth. It was oval shaped, and when he cleaned it with the bottom of his tunic and held it up to the light, he could see that it was not one color, but many. Paulo's eyes grew wide. As he saw the different colors that were reflected on the ground as the sun's light passed through it, he gasped.

"You have found a Legacy Stone!" Paulo cried out.

Ryu studied the stone in his hand. It was the size of a coin, and felt cold and smooth, like the blade of his knife back home. Indeed, it was a Legacy Stone. Ryu's older brother Roque had told him that Legacy Stones were shown only to those who had earned them. They could help one at any time during The Crossing, but one could not call upon their powers, they were revealed by the stone at a time of its choosing. Roque had told Ryu a story from his own Crossing, when the light from a Legacy stone had shown him the way in a place where the path had gotten dark.

Roque was much older than Ryu, and he was a Hunter. When Roque walked through the village, everyone would call to him, and smile or wave. Once, he had saved a little one who could not swim, and had fallen into The Wellspring River. And another time he had helped gather the flock when the strong wind from The Rains had opened the gate of their pen and they had run loose. Ryu knew that years ago Roque had helped save the other children on his Crossing when The Somethings had tried to trick them and

20

make them fall into a poisonous briar patch. Ryu had heard
stories from his aunts and uncles, his mother and father,
even his grandparents, of all the good things his older
brother had done on his Crossing. At the end, Roque had
been named a Champion.

Ryu greatly admired his older brother, and wanted to be
just like him one day. Soon, it would be Roque's time to
marry, and he would move away from their family cottage.
This made Ryu sad, for he knew that when Roque had a
family of his own, he would not see him every day as he
did now. Ryu loved to watch as his brother returned from
the hunt, and sometimes Roque would even let him help
clean his spears.

"Only Champions find Legacy Stones." Paulo said softly,
"You must be a Champion." He looked at Ryu in
amazement.

Ryu waved his hand, as if to sweep away The Yellow's
words. "We have only begun The Crossing," he answered
"It is too soon for anyone to be named a Champion." Ryu
had always been humble when others had given him praise,
or reward. He did not think of himself as anything special,
especially when compared to Roque. He tried to be the best
boy he could be, studied his lessons well, did his chores as
asked and helped others when they needed help. He tried to
be a good friend, and was well liked by the other children
in his lesson group. Ryu did not think these things made
him special, to him they were just The Right Thing to do.

He had learned the lesson of The Right Thing from his
mother when he was very young. Ryu's mother was a
village Elder, and often taught the weekly lesson from The
Book to the villagers who had met in The Village Center.

On the days when the rains kept everyone inside, she would read to him from The Book by the fire. The Book was a guide that had been written over many generations. It told stories of days long ago, and stories of the lessons learned by Those Who Have Passed. When someone had been lost, The Book could help them be found. When a child was unruly, the lessons of the book could help them understand the ways of the village. And at its center, at the very heart of The Book, was the lesson of The Right Thing.

"Do you know what the lesson of The Right Thing is trying to teach us Ryu?" his Mother had asked. He had been very young then, just having started to speak words himself, and he had shaken his head in answer.

"From the day we are born, we can feel The Right Thing. We have all felt its power in one way or another, even you my little one." His mother had come off of her rocking chair and sat facing Ryu on the woven rug by the hearth. Taking his face in her hands, she looked deep into his eyes as she spoke, "Every choice we make, every word we speak, every action we take, is watched by The Right Thing. It will touch us in some way, either in our minds, in our hearts, or even way down here in the bottom of your belly." She playfully poked Ryu's stomach and he giggled.

His mother had then become serious once again. "You must listen to what The Right Thing is telling you Ryu, you must always try to feel its message. In your life, there will be people, things and happenings that will try to drown out what The Right Thing is trying to say. Should you find yourself confused, you must listen hard, you must search within yourself and find the message of The Right Thing."

Ryu placed the stone in the pouch on his belt and tightened the drawstring. "We should go now," he said wiping the dirt from his hands onto his pants. "The Blue is far ahead and we should stay close should she need us again. Try to hurry." Stepping over the root that had tripped his friend, Ryu continued up the path.

Paulo followed, and was thoughtful as he moved to walk beside The Red. "She is your friend?" he asked, "The Blue?"

"Yes," Ryu answered, "Our families have known each other since before I was born."

"Is that why you look after her?" Paulo asked, "Because she is your friend?"

"I do not look after her," Ryu answered. "Brynn – I mean The Blue, she can look after herself. She is strong, and she is brave. She will do well on The Crossing."

"Then why should we catch up to her? Why should we hurry if she does not need us?"

"I did not say she does not need us," Ryu corrected him, "I said she could take care of herself."

They came to the turn in the path Brynn had seen earlier. As they went around the corner, the trees seemed to close in on them, and the path became quite dark. Ryu stopped for a moment to let his eyes adjust to the change in the light. He could hear The Yellow's breath quicken, and reached out his hand to find the boys.

"I am right here." Ryu said softly, and as his sight became clear, he could see Brynn a few lengths ahead. She had stopped and seemed to be staring at something to the right of the path. As they continued to walk, Ryu could see a puzzled look on Brynn's face and at once he knew that she had found the first Riddle.

He and Paulo were beside her now, and looked in the direction of her gaze. Between the trees they could see a giant boulder, the size of one of the cottages in their village. Etched into the stone, in letters as big as a grown man's hand, was the first Riddle. There was silence as the three read the words. After many moments, it was The Blue who spoke.

"I do not understand," Brynn said, her eyes desperately searching the words in the rock. "I do not understand what it means!"

Chapter 5

It blooms like the flower in the light of the morn
It began for you at the sound of the horn
You will need it now

Ryu was silent as he considered the Riddle. Paulo was also quiet at his side, trying to find an answer in the words before them.

"What blooms like a flower, other than a flower?" Brynn asked herself, the frustration swelling within her. "There is only the flower!" Here she was, at just the first Riddle of many, and she could not figure out its meaning. "I have always done very well with puzzles!" she blurted out.

The silence stretched out again as they all read each word etched into the rock carefully, weighing them as though they each were a stone held in their hands.

"It is not a puzzle," Paulo said softly. "The answer is different for each of us, therefore it can not be a puzzle."

"You understand what it means?" Brynn asked, looking at The Yellow with surprise. He was only a little boy.

"The Yellow is right," Ryu said smiling, "it is not a puzzle. The words only mean to show us something about ourselves that we may not have known before."

"I..." Brynn stammered, "I still do not understand."

"Love." Paulo blurted. "My mother has always said that love blossoms like a flower in the meadow."

"Love?" Brynn asked, confused. "What meaning does love have to The Crossing?"

"Not just love," Ryu answered again excitedly, "all of the things we feel grow within us like a flower. That is the message of this Riddle. For each of us, some new feeling blossomed at the beginning of The Crossing." He turned to look at them. "But we each must find for ourselves what that new feeling might be."

They all grew silent again, pondering this new question.

"Are we to stay here then, while we each find our answer?" asked Paulo, unsure of what he was to do next.

"No," said Brynn, "I think we are meant to continue on."

"Yes," agreed Ryu, "I believe you are right. I believe the answers will come as we walk." He paused for a moment and then turned to look at Brynn. "May we walk with you The Blue?" Ryu asked gently.

Brynn felt uneasy as she looked toward the path ahead which led into complete darkness. Perhaps it would be wiser for the three of them to walk together. "Yes," she said with certainty she did not really feel, "I think it would be wise for us to continue on together." And with that she turned and started back down the path of the Crossing, although now her steps were much, much slower.

They walked on side by side, very close to one another, for the path was just as narrow here as it had been before. As their eyes grew used to the darkness, they could see that the trees along the sides of the path had been replaced by large, rather angry looking bushes. The bushes bent over the path a few lengths above their heads, and grew into one another, forming a great tunnel. Their branches were thick, and had needle-like thorns. The leaves were long and thin, but plentiful. To fall into these bushes would have done great harm.

Looking above him, Ryu could see nothing but more of the same leaves and branches that were alongside him. There was no light let through to help them see what lay ahead. As the darkness seemed to close in, The Yellow once again reached for Ryu's hand. The air in the tunnel of trees was still and silent. The children had walked for quite some time when suddenly a warm breeze blew from somewhere ahead and sounds echoed around them.

"Do you hear that?" Ryu asked. It was music he was hearing. Soft, gentle music.

"Yes," Brynn said, "I hear it."

Paulo was frightened and could only nod.

It was the music of a lullaby, one that the mothers of their village sang often to newborn babes. In the tunnel of the harsh brush, with its intense blackness, it was difficult to tell which direction the music was coming from. One note seemed to come from in front, another from behind and yet another from above. As they walked, the music grew louder.

"Do you like my song?" asked a sweet voice from out of the darkness.

"Pardon me?" Brynn asked, stopping and looking all around her to try to see where the voice was coming from. "Where are you?"

"Do you like my song?" the voice asked again, this time sounding amused.

"Who are you?" Ryu asked boldly, holding Paulo's hand a little tighter. To him, the voice sounded as though it were coming from inside his head. "Are you a Something?"

Laughter that sounded like tinkling of wind chimes rang out. "A Something, a Nothing, these are the names that others before you have used. You may call me whatever you wish."

On the floor of the tunnel, half dozen lengths ahead, an enormous white snake slithered slowly toward them. Its body was as thick as a grown man's arm, and its pale skin had an iridescent glow. The children froze in fear, too scared to even turn and run. With its large yellow eyes, the creature seemed to study them as it stopped only a few lengths in front of them and curled itself into ring, its head poised sharply in midair.

"Do you like my song?" the voice asked again, only this time it seemed less amused.

"Could it be that this snake is speaking to me in my mind?" Ryu thought to himself as he pulled Paulo close under his arm.

The snake nodded his head slowly as its gaze fell directly upon Ryu. "Yes, it is I, and I will ask you once more – do you like my song?"

"It is a song my mother sings to comfort me when I am not well." Paulo said softly, almost beneath his breath, not wishing to anger this ominous creature before them.

"Ah, so then you know this song." The snake began to sway its head ever so slightly back and forth, as if in time to the notes.

"Yes, we all know this song," Brynn said, a slight tremor in her voice, "Why is it important?"

"Do you know the words?" the voice asked, sounding amused once again. "Do you know the words to my song?"

As I tuck you in this night
This is your left foot, this is your right
As I tuck you in this night
This is your left hand, this is your right
As I tuck you in this night,
I will kiss your left cheek and I will kiss your right
Snuggle in, snuggle in
Snuggle in tight.

Paulo sang the words quietly as he had done many times while helping his mother put the little ones to sleep.

The snake's yellow eyes glowed brightly. "Very good, very good indeed. Now, which do you choose?"

"Pardon me?" Brynn asked again, very confused.

"Which do you choose?" the snake asked turning to look toward where it had come from. A faint light from above, sunlight poking its way through a small hole in the bushes, shone down on the path a few dozen or so lengths ahead. "Which do you choose, left or right?"

With this light, the three could see that the path split into two paths up ahead. There were two distinct tunnels of dense bushes, one to the left, and one to the right. The one on the left was as dark as the one they were in now, but there was a soft glow coming from the path on the right.

The snake turned to look at them once more. "I will ask again, and do choose wisely. Will you take the left path, or will you take the right?"

Chapter 6

The three each looked to the paths ahead. "How will we know which is the right one?" the Red asked.

One again, the laughter of the voice chimed through the silence. "Right, wrong, left or right? How does one make any choice that is before them?" asked the snake as its eyes seemed to grow larger and glow with amber light, "Why, by choosing of course!" And then just as suddenly as it had appeared, the large white snake disappeared right before their eyes.

Brynn closed and then opened her eyes to make them used to the darkness again.

"Your eyes will see in a moment." Ryu assured Paulo.

When their eyes could see, the glow of the path on the right was brighter. Its light was also cast on the entrance of the other path, which showed no light at all, only a dense blackness.

"We must move on," Ryu said after a moment. "We must choose a path."

"I will take the right path." Brynn said decidedly and started on her way.

Ryu grabbed her quickly by the hand, "Wait, Brynn – I mean The Blue. How do you know it is safe?"

"There is light," Brynn said matter-of-factly. "It is much safer to walk in light than it is to walk in darkness." And she turned to go again.

Ryu would not let go of her hand. "Fire is not always safe, and yet it is light. Please Brynn, we should think more about this choice."

Bryn pulled her hand out of Ryu's grasp. "I do not need to think more about it, Ryu", she said sharply. "I will take the path to the right, and that is that!" Bryn walked briskly toward the glow of the path she had chosen.

Ryu wanted to chase after her, to make her stay with them, but he knew she would not change her mind. Once Brynn had made up her mind to do something, it was precisely what she would do, even if it was the wrong thing to do.

Ryu remembered a time, a few seasons before, when he and Brynn had been coming back from a day of playing out in The West Woods. They had stayed to play one more game of Hideaway while the other children had already gone home. It was getting late, almost supper time, and Brynn was in a hurry to get back to cook a meal for her mother.

"We shall cut through The Dancing Field," she had said. "Then we will make it in time."

Ryu had shaken his head, "No Brynn, it is forbidden to walk in The Dancing Field. The elders have spoken many times of The Biters who live in the grasses."

"We are very fast runners Ryu," Brynn had assured him. "We will run so fast that The Biters will not even see our feet to bite them!" She had smiled and turned in the direction of the field, but Ryu shook his head again.

"No Brynn, I will not go through The Dancing Field, I will stay on the path home."

"Fine," said Brynn angrily, "I will go myself!"

Ryu watched as she made her way through the trees toward The Dancing Field. He had hurried along the path that lead to the village, and had reached his family's cottage just as his mother was putting the evening meal on the table. His brother and father were seated waiting to eat.

"Thank the stars," Ryu's mother had said as she put her arms around him. "You have made it home safe!" Letting him go, she motioned to the table, "Sit now and eat with your father and brother. I must go to help tend to Brynn."

"Brynn?" Ryu asked anxiously, "What has happened to Brynn?"

"Silly girl," Roque had said with a shake of his head.

"She crossed through The Dancing Field," his mother answered as she wrapped her shawl around her shoulders, "And her feet and legs are covered in The Biters stings."

"I...I...I tried to stop her." Ryu stammered.

His father stopped eating. "You were with her?" he had had asked, and guilt washed over Ryu like a wave. He knew he should have tried harder to stop her, to make her take the safe path home.

"Yes," Ryu answered quietly. "We were playing in The West Woods."

"Well it is a good thing you had enough sense to heed the warnings of the Elders!" said his father and continued his meal.

"Will she be alright?" Ryu had asked his mother then.

"Yes my son," his mother had answered with a sigh, "with salve and wrappings, Brynn should be healed in a few days." She lifted her medicine bag off its hook by the door and turned to go. As she opened the door, she stopped and looked back at her youngest son, "I am proud of you Ryu." she had said with a small smile.

Ryu remembered feeling confused. Why was his mother proud? It was because he had let Brynn go on by herself that she had gotten hurt. She should not be proud, he had failed his friend.

His mother could see his confused expression and hers was warm in return. "I am proud of you Ryu for listening hard, and hearing what The Right Thing was telling you."

The Right Thing. Ryu was desperately searching for its message within himself now. At the same time he worried for Brynn. It was not wise to make a decision such as this as quickly as she had, and he knew that sometimes things were not always what they seemed.

"Which way shall we go The Red?" Paulo asked.

Ryu could see the fear in the boys eyes as they looked up at his. Ryu smiled as he looked down on him. Paulo looked so small and helpless standing there and Ryu knew he was counting on him to lead the way. "Please, call me Ryu" he said with a smile and patted the boys head. "We are friends now."

"But the rules say that we must use the colors as our names." Paulo said, even though he was very honored that this boy, this Champion, would want to be his friend.

"I think that rule is meant for those on The Crossing who are not friends. You and I, we are friends."

Not wanting to disagree, Paulo nodded his head with a grin. "Alright Ryu. My name is Paulo." He said and then remembered all too quickly the problem at hand, "Which path shall we take?"

Ryu thought for a moment. "It would be easy to choose the path on the right, for as Brynn said, it is much easier to walk in the light. But we do not know where that light is coming from, or how long it will last." He pointed to the path on the left, "There is no light at the beginning of that path, but we do not know if there may be light further on."

A scream broke through his thoughts. "Help, help me, please!" It was Brynn.

"It is The Blue," Paulo shouted. Without hesitation, both he and Ryu started to run towards Brynn's cries.

"It would seem," said Ryu, his heart pounding with each step, "that our choice has been made for us."

Chapter 7

They reached the entrance to the tunnel in moments and the light that shone within it blinded them. Ryu stopped to get his bearings and could see that the light was coming from above where a hole in the dense bush allowed the sunlight through. The hole was not large, but the sun was sitting just right in the sky, and its rays were reflected in a small pool of water below. Beyond that one small area of light the darkness of the outer tunnel continued.

"Ryu, someone, please help me!" Brynn was shouting but her words, which were full with fear, seemed to be coming from very far away.

"Where are you Brynn?" Ryu shouted back. "I cannot see past the patch of light."

"I am..."

Brynn's words were drowned out by the sound of rushing water.

"It sounds like a river." Paulo said, looking into the black ahead.

"Brynn?" Ryu called again. If there was an answer, they could not hear it. The roar of passing water was very loud now.

"We must try to find her." Ryu said, hurrying as he walked toward the light. As he passed through it and the darkness on the other side surrounded him, he could feel the path slanting downward under his feet. As his eyes grew familiar to the dark once again, he could see that the path dropped away quite suddenly. "Stop!" he cried to Paulo, who had been following carefully behind him. "The path falls here."

Paulo stopped and examined the steep drop. "The Blue must have fallen," he said looking over the edge. "I can not see how far it goes."

"Give me your belt," Ryu said as he was untying his own. "I will tie them together and lower you down. You can see how far it is to the bottom, and then I will know whether or not it is safe to jump."

"But…I" Paulo hesitated, "I cannot hold on to a rope for long." He lowered his head. "I cannot even swing out over the pond as the other children do."

Ryu looked at the boy hard. "I know you can do this," he said urgently. "Brynn needs our help, she may even be hurt. We have to get to her quickly. Please Paulo, you must try!" He could see the boy was afraid. "If you believe you can do it," he said meeting the boy's eyes, "then you will do it."

"Alright," Paulo said, removing his belt, "I will try."

Tying the two ropes together and making a loop at either end for each of them to hold, Ryu dug two holes in the dirt where he could steady his feet. "Put the loop around your wrist and hold tight to the rope, that way it will not slip from your hands," he instructed Paulo. He had to speak loudly now, over the thunderous sound of the water. "Turn, and hang your feet down. When you let go, I will lower you with the rope."

Paulo wrapped the rope around his arm as Ryu had said, and sat on the edge of the ledge. Turning, he pushed himself so that he was facing Ryu and his legs swung down over the edge. Taking a deep breath he said, "I am ready."

Ryu dug his feet into the holes he had made and leaned back on them. "Ready," he said in answer.

Paulo let his body fall away from the ledge. Ryu stood firm, and slowly let the slack of rope out. "Can you see anything?" he managed to call out through clenched teeth.

Looking down, Paulo could see nothing. "No, I can not," he yelled as the rope lowered him further and further. "But I can hear the water. It is very close." Although his arms ached and the rope rubbed his skin, Paulo did not feel as though he would fall. He knew Ryu would not let him.

A moment later, Paulo felt the tips of his feet touch ground. "I have reached the bottom!" he exclaimed excitedly, having to shout over the sound of the rushing water. Ryu figured he had lowered him about six or so lengths. He could easily jump down that distance.

As Paulo got his footing below, Ryu walked to the edge and called down, "What can you see now?"

"It is dark," Paulo answered loudly, "I still can not see anything!" Taking a step forward, too late he realized that he had been standing at the top of a sharp slope and he began to tumble forward. "Ryu!" he called out.

The slack of rope Ryu had been holding began to quickly disappear below as Paulo rolled down the incline. In seconds the rope was pulled taunt, and Ryu held on with all of his might. The rope had stopped Paulo's fall, but it had pulled Ryu to the edge of the drop and he was struggling to hold his balance. "Paulo", he called, "are you alright?!"

Paulo had landed face down in the dirt and his wrist was raw from where the rope had burned him, but he was alright. "Yes," he shouted back, "I fell down a slope. It is very steep. I think the river may be at the bottom."

"Can you climb back up?" asked Ryu. "When you are sturdy, I can jump down and we can go down the slope together."

"Yes, I think so," Paulo said as he pulled himself to his knees. Crawling very slowly, he made his way back up to where he had started to fall. "I am at the top!" he called to Ryu. "You must be careful when you jump down. If you lose your footing, you will fall as I did!"

"Stand to the side if you can," Ryu said as he positioned himself. "I am coming down!" And with that he pushed off from the ledge and jumped down into the darkness.

He had landed on a soft spot in the dirt, and Ryu's feet started to give way beneath him. He rocked backward, off balance. Paulo, whose eyes had by now adjusted to the dim light, quickly reached out and grabbed onto Ryu's tunic, steadying him.

Ryu let out a sigh of relief. "Thank you for catching me my friend."

It was then that the Legacy Stone began to glow. "Look!" Paulo said, pointing to Ryu's pouch. Ryu looked down, and saw the light coming from within it. Releasing the drawstring, he pulled the stone from the pouch and held it up.

The light that came from the Legacy Stone was brighter than a torch and now he and Paulo could easily see the cave around them, the slope before them, as well as the river that flowed at its bottom. Its waters were only half as wide as those of Wellspring River which ran passed their village at its southern border, but they were moving quickly, as though the river had been flooded. Moving slowly, with very small steps, the boys made their way down the slope. At the bottom, the dark water was no more than a length in front of them.

"Someone! Please! Help me!" Brynn's voice came from the right. Turning to hold the Legacy Stone in that direction, they could see her now, in the middle of the river. She was clinging to a jutting rock, and they could see she was fighting the current that was trying to take her with it on its way.

"I cannot hold much longer!" Brynn cried, having to turn her face away from the waves made by the water hitting the rock she clung to. "Help me, please!

Chapter 8

"Hold on Brynn!" Ryu called as he and Paulo made their way toward her, trying not to fall into the dark, angry looking water themselves. There were solid rock walls on both sides of the river, with only a narrow strip of dirt between them and the edge of it.

"How will we get to her?" Paulo shouted to Ryu, hurrying to keep up with the older boy. A few moments later, when they had reached the spot where Brynn was holding on to the rock in the middle of the raging water, they saw that she was at least eight lengths away from them.

Ryu gathered the rope that was still tied around his waist. Turning, he reached as high as he could and placed the Legacy Stone on a small ledge, its glow still bright enough to light the entire cave. As he searched the wall of rock before him with both his hands and his eyes he asked urgently, "Can you swim?"

"Wh..what..wh..why..well, yes." Paulo stammered, "What is it you wish to do?"

"Ah, here," Ryu exclaimed. He had found a place in the rock where it had cracked and jutted away from itself. He quickly slid the loop of rope, the one he hade made for Paulo's hand when he had lowered him from the ledge, around the protruding rock. He pulled the rope hard to make sure it would hold. "Good," he said, turning to Paulo. "I will walk back a few lengths and go into the river there. I will swim toward the middle as fast as I can, and the river will take me down toward Brynn. Once I reach her, I will have her hold on to me, and I will swim with her back to the bank. The rope will hold, but I will not be able to pull both Brynn and I back up using it, the current is too strong. You must pull on the rope and help guide us back to shore."

Paulo, once again, looked afraid. What if he was not strong enough to help? The river looked so dark, and its waters rushed so fast, how could anyone swim through it? Ryu grabbed the boy by the shoulders and stared into his eyes, "Do you understand?"

"Yes," he answered firmly, meeting Ryu's eyes and feeling a little braver. Over Ryu's shoulder, Paulo could see Brynn struggling in the water as the waves got higher. It would not be long before the river swept her away. "We must hurry!" he said as he took his place just ahead of where the rope was anchored to the wall.

Ryu gave a quick nod before turning back toward the slope where they had come from. He walked a few lengths before slowly wading into the river. The water was ice cold, and it was flowing so fast that he could barely stand. He had only gone about a length in when the bottom dropped away, and he was forced to start swimming. Punching the water with each stroke to break through the waves, he knew he had to swim as hard as he could or he would not make it to the middle where Brynn was.

The river swelled suddenly, lifting Ryu up and dropping him down half a length passed where Brynn was holding on. The rope was pulled tight. He had missed her. Knowing it would be impossible to swim up river against the current, Ryu pushed himself toward the shore.

Paulo grabbed the slack as Ryu came closer and pulled on the rope with all his might. He could hear the pounding of his heart in his ears, which seemed even louder than the noise of the rushing river. Ryu made it to the ledge at the side of the river finally and lifted himself out of the water.

"Ryu!" Brynn called frantically.

"Hold on Brynn!" Ryu called back, "I will try again!"

"Hurry Ryu!" Paulo urged, "She can not hold on much longer!"

Dripping wet and shivering from the cold water, Ryu made his way back up the river. This time he went two lengths further than he had the first try before making his way into the water. He used the ledge to push himself out toward the center and kicked his feet as fast as he could. Thankfully the water was somewhat calmer, and although the current was still strong, he was able to make his way across the river slowly.

Finally just as the tide was going to take him passed her again, Ryu reached out his arm and caught hold of Brynn's outstretched hand. Paulo could see Ryu wrap one arm around The Blue, as she put her arms around his neck. As she let go, they both were swept downriver, pulling the rope tight once again. Ryu swam as hard as he could toward the shore, with Brynn holding on around his neck. As they got closer, the rope gained some slack and Paulo wrapped it around his hand and started to pull. As the waves pounded him, Ryu struggled to pull them through the water. His muscles were starting to tire and the icy water was making them ache even more. But slowly, with the help of Paulo pulling the rope, they were making their way to shore. Just a little farther and they would be safe.

Then, as they were little more than two lengths away, the rope that had been Ryu and Brynn's anchor snapped. Still holding the rope, Paulo cried out as the weight of them pulled him off his feet and sent him splashing into the water. Sputtering, he fought his way to the surface and tried to gain his bearings. He could see Ryu and Brynn being pulled down the river ahead, but the waves kept smashing over him, and he could not call out to them.

As the children flowed further down the river away from it, the light from the Legacy Stone faded, and the darkness started to close in around them. Feeling a tug, Paulo suddenly realized that the rope was still wrapped around his wrist and that the other end was still tied to Ryu. He held on tight. It was a small comfort that he was connected to his friend, as the tide swept him away into the darkness and he desperately tried to keep his head above the water.

Chapter 9

Ryu fought the current, trying to swim toward the side of the river, but it was no use. With Brynn holding on to him, and the cold water making his muscles very tired, he felt as though he were swimming in mud. As much as his body wished to stop fighting the will of the water, in his heart he knew he must not give up. He must get them to safety.

The water was slowing now and Ryu could see light up ahead. Hope washed over him, and he kicked his feet hard. When they got closer, he could see that the cave ended, and the sun was shining down. With one final push, the river spit them out of the cave from which it flowed and into calmer water. Lush grass lined both sides of the river and there was a small inlet a dozen or so lengths up on the left hand side. Ryu swam toward it. Brynn saw the cove as well, and letting go of Ryu's neck, she swam the rest of the way on her own.

It was then that Ryu felt the tug of the rope around his waist and realized that he must still be tied to Paulo. Looking back toward the cave, Ryu saw him bobbing up and down in the water. Paulo was very small and very light, and even though the current had slowed, it was pulling him around in the water so that he looked like a fish struggling to free itself from a line.

Ryu gathered what strength he had left, raced to shore and pulled himself up beside where Brynn lay, trying to catch her breath. Panic gripped him when he could not see Paulo for a moment, but seconds later his head reappeared above the water.

"Help me pull him in!" Ryu pleaded to Brynn.

She saw The Yellow struggling in the water and quickly grabbed the rope behind Ryu. Together they pulled, and Paulo did his best to use swim toward them with his free hand. When he finally reached the shore, they pulled him up onto the grass, and all three collapsed in a heap. Rolling off one another moments later, the children lay panting, as the seriousness of what had happened weighed down on them. The bright sun felt warm on their cold wet skin, and the thick grass felt soft underneath them. They could hear a bird chirping somewhere in the distance. Brynn started to cry softly.

"I am so sorry," she said quietly, sitting up. "Had I listened to you Ryu, we would have chosen the other path. We would have stayed together." Brynn was crying harder now. "You saved me. You and the Yellow were so brave. Had you not come, I…I…" Her sobs were filled with deep regret. Ryu said nothing as he sat and wrapped his arms around her. He hugged her tight, and let her cry.

When the tears slowed and she could speak, Brynn's voice trembled. "Thank you," she managed to say. "Thank you, Ryu. Thank you the…"

"Paulo," the young boy interrupted, sitting up and looking at Brynn sheepishly. "My name is Paulo."

"Thank you Paulo." Wiping her tears away, Brynn gave him a small smile. "Thank you for saving me." Paulo could feel his cheeks turn red. Looking down, he concentrated on untangling the rope around his wrist.

"And I thank you both," Paulo said hastily, after freeing himself, "for pulling me out of the river." He rubbed his wrists where the rope had left raised welts.

"You were doing just fine," Ryu said as he gave Paulo's arm a playful nudge with his own. "You did not really need our help." They exchanged a knowing smirk.

"When I was holding on to the rock in the river, there was a light in the cave." Brynn said confused.

"Ryu found a Legacy Stone!" Paulo said excitedly. "He is a Champion!"

"Yes," Brynn said sweetly as she looked to her friend, "I knew Ryu would be a Champion."

Embarrassed by their attention, Ryu stood. As he untied Paulo's belt from his own and handed it to him, he reached for the compass around his neck so that he might get his bearings and figure out in which direction they needed to continue on. The compass was not there.

"It would seem that the river has claimed our only means of finding our way home," Ryu said pointing to where the compass should be.

"How will we find our village?' Brynn asked, feeling a little afraid.

Ryu stopped and thought for a moment, "The cave is there," he said pointing at the angry water rushing out of the mouth of it, "And the path we came from must be behind it."

Brynn rose to her feet as well, cringing slightly as the feeling in her scraped hands returned and looked in the direction Ryu was speaking of. "We should go back, and find the path," she said.

Paulo looked up in the sky as he retied the rope belt around his waist. The sun was almost directly overhead. "We do not need to go all the way back," he said excitedly. He pointed to the left beyond the cave, "The sun started in the sky there, where we started. Now it is moving toward the middle of the sky and going toward there," he said, motioning to the field of tall grasses behind them. "Our village is to the West. We just need to follow the sun."

Brynn turned to look at the field with its tall thick grasses, and fear started to grow in her belly. She could remember the sting of The Biters that had attacked her legs the day she had cut across The Dancing Field as though it had happened only yesterday. It had taken many days for the pain to subside and the swelling to go down. She did not want to encounter The Biters ever again. Ryu could see the apprehension on her face and knew what she was afraid of.

"There is no other way Brynn," Ryu said gently. "Even if we go back toward the cave, we must still walk through the grasses." He could see her fear growing. "I will carry you on my back if you'd like," he offered nobly.

"Look!" Paulo exclaimed then, standing and pointing to the field behind them. The grasses had parted, revealing a narrow flat path leading in the direction the sun was heading. All three knew it had not been there before. As they stood staring in amazement, a small bird, no bigger than a stone they would skip into the pond, appeared at the beginning of the path. It was the same color brown as many of the other birds who lived in the trees around their village, but its wings fluttered so fast they could hardly see them. It hovered there, as though it were waiting.

"I think it means for us to follow it," Paulo said excitedly. "Yes," replied Ryu, "I think you are right."

The little brown bird, who continued to hang in the air over the entrance to this new path, seemed to be watching them patiently.

Not wanting to make a hasty decision like she had when choosing the path that had lead to the river, Brynn asked, "How do we know it is safe?"

Ryu was silent for a moment. "There is no way to know," he said finally. "We know that we can not walk down the river, it leads away from where we need to go," he reasoned. "If we go back toward the cave, we must walk through the tall grasses, and there may be The Biters hiding in them." Brynn shuddered at the thought of them.

"That means to follow this bird is really the only choice," Paulo said finishing Ryu's thinking.

"Yes. It is the only safe choice," Brynn agreed, adding, "And this time, we will all be together." She looked at the boys, both grateful to them for all they had done, and grateful to be with them now.

And as if understanding their words, the little brown bird turned and started to fly slowly down the path.

Chapter 10

The path in the field was narrower than the path through the bushes had been, and it forced the children to walk single file. After talking for a moment, the children had agreed that Brynn would walk first with Paulo in the middle. Ryu, who would be considered the strongest because he was the eldest, would protect the group at the rear as was the custom of the hunting parties in their village.

The path was straight, other than where it curved around large rocks now and again, and was pounded quite flat. The grasses on either side were as high as Brynn's chest, and she nervously looked back and forth, praying that The Biters did not live in them. The little bird that seemed to be their guide stayed a few lengths in front of the children, and now and again Brynn would look up to make sure it was still there. Having it fly with them made her feel a bit safer somehow.

Brynn was thinking about her fall into the river. She knew she was lucky not to have been seriously hurt, or even… Her cheeks flushed with embarrassment as she thought of how foolish she had been. She had chosen the wrong path because she had wanted to hurry, wanted to be the first of them to finish The Crossing. She knew she had acted without thinking things through and had put Ryu and Paulo, as well as herself, in danger.

"You must always consider the consequences of your actions Brynn and how they may affect others." It was her father's voice in her head again.

*She had been just three years old and had been playing
with the other young children in The Daisy Meadow. She
was playing on the see saw with Gryfyn, a boy who was
also three, when a beautiful Pink Star had flown close to
them. Gryfyn had been up in the air on his end of the wood
plank when Brynn had decided to jump off of her end and
chase the pretty insect. The young boy let out a wail as he
came crashing down, hitting the ground hard.*

*Many parents came rushing, and when they got him back to
his cottage, it was discovered that he had broken a bone in
one of his fingers. Her mother had taken her home
immediately and Brynn remembered being afraid that she
would be punished. She was surprised when her father,
instead of making her recite passages from The Book, took
her to The River Fish Pond. Kneeling, he had picked up a
small flat stone and skipped it across the water. Brynn
watched as it jumped many times before sinking to the
bottom. Her father had been a very good stone skipper.*

*"What did I just do?" he had asked her. Brynn wondered if
he might be tricking her.*

Smiling she answered, "You threw a stone father."

"Is that all?" he asked, his face serious.

*Brynn realized he was not joking, and her smile faded.
"Umm..."*

"What did I do before I threw the stone?"

*There was silence as Brynn tried to figure out what exactly
her father was asking. He sighed as he looked at her
standing there, so young and innocent.*

"I made choices," he said sternly, "I chose to throw a stone and I chose which stone I would throw. You chose to chase the Pink Star and to get off the see saw before Gryfyn was safe." He paused a moment before continuing. "Everything we do touches everything, and everyone around us Brynn."

Brynn's father reached down and plucked another stone from the ground. "If I choose this stone to skip, I may change many things. This could be the rock that a Blue Bug lives under," he said, turning it over in his hand, "or where a Mud Beetle has laid her eggs. Maybe it is the favorite rock of a Water Lizard, and now that I have moved it, he will no longer be able to use it to sun himself on." He skipped the stone he was holding across the pond as he had done with the one before.

"And what have I changed now?" he asked after it had disappeared from sight, although this time Brynn knew that he was not expecting her to answer. "Now, I may have changed the path of a leaf floating on the water that a Whistle Bird could use to build her nest, or even killed a Gliding Spider as it tried to make its way across the pond. And what happens once the stone reaches the bottom? Does it trap a Sliver Fish who lives there? Or maybe it will land on her babies, crushing them."

Brynn looked at him in dismay. "Oh father!" she cried.

His tone was gentle as he looked into Brynn's eyes then. "Every action we take has consequences, and sometimes more than one outcome. You must consider all of the things and all of the people your actions may affect before you do something. If you do not wish harm to come to you, or to

anyone or anything around you, you must think of all the
things that may happen because of what you choose to do."
Brynn felt sorry again that she had put Ryu and Paulo in
harms way. She had been in such a hurry, wanting to be the
first one to finish The Crossing, she did not stop to think
about her choice. It had been unwise not to stay with them
and figure out together which path to take. She had been
stubborn and unwilling to listen to Ryu because she thought
she could make her own decisions, that she did not need
him to tell her what to do.

"Ryu is your friend," a voice in her head spoke. Was it her
father's voice she heard now? "He only wants to help you.
Paulo is your friend as well. Think of all he did to save
you."

Brynn knew now that she did not have to continue on The
Crossing alone, in fact it would be silly to do so. She did
not have to face the Somethings, the Nothings or figure out
The Riddles by herself. She could ask for help if she
needed to. The Crossing did not have to be like her life
back in the village, where she felt so alone, with so many
responsibilities. Ryu and Paulo were with her now. She
could share this journey with her friends.

> *It blooms like the flower in the light of the morn*
> *It began for you at the sound of the horn*
> *You will need it now*

"That is it!" Brynn said out loud excitedly.

"That is what?' Paulo asked, looking around to see what
she was speaking of.

Brynn's smile was wide as she turned to answer him, "I am sorry, I did not mean to burst out like that." She felt as though a great weight had been lifted from her heart. "I was speaking to myself."

Paulo nodded, and met her smile with one of his own as he walked carefully behind her. Just by hearing the relief in her voice and seeing the grin on her face, he knew that Brynn had found her answer to the first Riddle. He knew too, because only a few moments earlier, as he walked behind the older girl he had helped save from the river, he had found his own answer.

Chapter 11

Paulo had four younger siblings; his sister Pia was six, his brother Piero was four, and the twins, Patia and Pirtia were two. His mother also watched over a few children, who were still too young to go for lessons, while their mothers and fathers worked in the village center. With all the little ones around, the cottage was bustling with activity from early in the morning until the sun kissed the horizon good night.

As the eldest of the children, when they arrived home from their lessons, Paulo and Pia would help their mother prepare the meals and take care of the younger ones. Although he did not mind all of the noise and laughter, sometimes Paulo would sneak away for a few moments during Sleep Time and climb the trees around the village to find a quiet place where he could be by himself and hear his own thoughts.

"You are a thinker," his father would tell him on their fishing trips to The River Fish Pond, *"just as I am."*

Paulo knew his father was considered a very important man in their village, although his manner was such that it appeared he either did not know it, or it did not matter to him. He was head of The Sciences Council, and had designed the water system which now carried fresh water from The Crystal Wells right into each of the cottages in the village. Families no longer had to walk back and forth to the Wells to get water to drink, or to cook their food, or even water their animals. Because of the time this had saved, the villagers had begun work on a new system of roads, which would make it easier to visit the neighboring villages. Paulo's father was regarded as a visionary, and a man of great intellect.

Paulo thought that everyone expected him to follow in his father's footsteps, studying the sciences and someday joining The Council. He knew his father was right, he was "a thinker", and his lessons had always been easy for him. He was fascinated by science, always enjoyed looking at his father's latest plans and drawings and took pleasure in hearing him explain how his latest project would work.

Science, however, was not where Paulo's heart was trying to lead him. He would leave the cottage early on those few mornings he was not needed to help and sit up in the trees before going to his lessons. If he was lucky, and the sun had not yet appeared in the sky, he could watch the hunters head out toward The West Forest. Some days, when his lessons had ended early enough, he would steal a few moments before heading home to watch as they emerged from the forest, dragging the carcasses of that day's prey behind them.

The hunters were dirty and sweaty, and Paulo could see the deep scratches on their arms from where they had come too close to the sharp brush. But he could also hear the excitement, and the pride in their voices, as the recounted the days hunt. It was these stories that made his heart sing. When Paulo closed his eyes he could imagine the hunters, with their bows tied to the harnesses on their backs running through the trees as fast as the wind and yet as quiet as a whisper. He could imagine their muscles straining as they lifted heavy rocks, working swiftly to make blinds, places to hide where the animals would not see them. He could see the hunters in his mind, drawing their bows and taking aim when they sighted their prey.

Each hunter said The Giving Payer right before ending an animal's life. Paulo knew the words by heart.

You give your body to provide food for our homes.
I give your spirit the freedom to find The Great Forever.
This is The Giving.

The biggest and tallest of the boys and girls in his village were asked to be hunters. It took great strength to build the rock blinds and to carry home the days catch. The hunter's long legs carried them quickly over great distances, and made hurdling over the fallen trees in the forest much easier. The hunt could be dangerous. Many had been attacked by wild animals and had tumbled into steep raveens. A few had even been lost when the Strong Winds had come without warning and falling trees had claimed their lives.

Paulo stared at Brynn's back as he followed cautiously behind her. "When she is older, she could be a hunter," he had thought to himself. To him Brynn seemed very tall, and he knew she was very strong. She had held on to the rock in the river much longer than he could have, even with her injured hands. He did not think he would ever be big enough or powerful enough to be a part of the hunt.

"But you held on to the rope as Ryu lowered you down from the ledge. You stopped him from falling down the slope and you swam through the current in the river. You have made it this far," a voice in his head spoke, answering his doubts. *"You did those things Paulo. Why is it then that you could not be a hunter?"*

At that moment he had looked up and saw that the little brown bird was looking behind at him as it flew, still leading the way down the path. He wondered if the voice in his head was that of the bird, talking to him as the snake in the tunnel had spoken to the three of them, or if it was his own mind asking the question.

Why not? If he could drop from a ledge into darkness, stop his friend from falling in the raging river and help save Brynn from its icy waters, why could he not be a hunter when he was old enough? He thought, and thought, but no answer came, no answer at all. Why could he not be a hunter? There was no reason he could not. And that is when he knew his answer to the first riddle.

"Look there!" Brynn had stopped and was pointing to a circle of large boulders that was a few lengths to the right of the path. The children could see a banquet of food had been laid out in the center of it, and a drinking well was just behind it. The little brown bird flew over to this resting area and hovered above it for a few moments. Then he quickly nodded his head, as if to say good-bye, turned and flew swiftly away.

"I am starving!" Ryu said as he hurried toward the food on the make-shift table, which was in fact the trunks of two large trees pushed together and covered with a plank. Ryu sank to his knees as he reached for the freshly roasted meat with one hand and the sweet ripened Langa fruit with the other. Brynn quickly joined him.

Paulo's thirst was far greater than his hunger, and he went straight to the well, which was behind the largest of the circle of six boulders. Dropping the bucket down into the water, he saw that wooden cups had been left on a rock beside the well. As he reached for one, his eyes were drawn to a large flat rock a couple of lengths away that was so shiny and white, it reflected the sun's rays and appeared to glow. After winding the bucket back up from the bottom of the well and drinking two cups of the cold refreshing water, Paulo went to have a closer look at the mysterious rock. He had not taken more than a few steps when he saw the writing etched into its flat surface.

"Ryu, Brynn," he called out, "I have found the second Riddle!" Both of them dropped the food in their hands, quickly got to their feet and rushed to where their friend stood, pondering the words in front of him.

You must choose what to believe
Your eyes and ears, they can deceive
You cannot win.

Chapter 12

Brynn, Ryu and Paulo stood staring at the ominous riddle. Before any of them could speak a word, they heard a desperate cry.

"Help, someone please help me! I am trapped!" It was a girl's voice, and seemed to be coming from a large group of briar bushes a few dozen lengths directly in front of them.

"Please, I cannot get out!"

The children rushed to the group of bushes. At first, they did not see anyone, but moving around to the back they could see a girl, about their age, and she was tangled in the branches of a very large briar bush.

"Thank goodness!" she said upon seeing them. "I tripped on a stone and fell into this bush. Please help me!" Her large blue eyes were rimmed with tears, and Ryu moved quickly to where she was.

"Do not struggle," he instructed her gently, as he examined her position and tried to figure out the best way to free her. She was a small thin child, and she looked so helpless in that huge bush, like a fly caught in a spider's web. The girl was crouched down, and the sharp thorns were wound in her long blonde hair. Her arms had somehow been trapped in the branches above her head.

Ryu turned to Brynn and Paulo, "It is not the poisonous kind," he told them, "but we will have to snap the branches one by one."

Moving beside him, the friends began to slowly and carefully break off the branches of the bush. It was dry, and the branches were brittle, so it was not difficult to break them. They had to be careful however, so as not to prick themselves or the little girl with the thorns. After several minutes, they had broken away all of the branches, and Ryu offered the girl his hand so she could pull herself up and out of the bush.

"Oh thank you!" she cried, rubbing her arms where the thorns had pressed so hard that they had left deep red marks. "I do not know what I would have done if you had not come along." She gave them a shy smile as she wiped away her tears, "My name is L'Har."

"I am Ryu. This is Brynn," Ryu said nodding his head toward where Brynn stood, "and this is Paulo."

Paulo could barely look up to meet L'Har's eyes. She was the prettiest girl he had ever seen. Her golden hair was long and curly, and her eyes were the clear blue of a cloud free sky. Her smooth alabaster skin made her features appear as though they had been carved out of marble. Her beautiful smile was accented by two deep dimples in her cheeks. When L'Har spoke, her voice sounded like music to Paulo's ears. She wore the almost the same uniform of The Crossing as they did, only her arm band was black.

"Hello Paulo," L'Har said with a little wave and sweet smile.

"What are you doing here?" Brynn asked, maybe a little too sharply. She was surprised by her tone, she had not meant to sound rude. There was just something about this girl, who had appeared out of nowhere, that made her feel anxious.

L'Har's smile faded as she turned to Brynn. "I was on The Crossing with two others from my village, but we got separated," she replied, politely enough. "I was looking for them when I tripped on a large stone and fell into the bush."

"Which village are you from?" Ryu asked.

"We came from The South Village," she replied, her smile returning as she looked at him.

"We were just eating," Brynn said, and then to make up for her earlier rudeness asked, "Would you care to join us?"

The little blonde girl seemed to consider the question for a moment before answering, "I have already eaten, but I will sit with you if that is alright."

"Yes!" The word burst from Paulo's lips before he even had a chance to consider it. His cheeks grew red. "I, I mean, yes, please join us." He turned quickly and hurried back toward the circle of boulders. L'Har giggled quietly as she followed him.

Hunger had gotten the best of the three friends, and nothing was said as they kneeled and devoured the delicious food before them. L'Har pulled thorns from her hair as she politely sat on a nearby rock and waited.

When they were finished eating, Ryu turned to L'Har. "What happened to those you were travelling with?"

"There was a large tree in the center of the path," she answered, "so large that it split the path in two. You could only go around to the right of it, or to the left of it. The path on either side was narrow, so that only one could walk. Timar, he is the oldest, said he would take Voler, she is a year younger than I am, on the left path. He said I should take the right path, and we would meet up again on the other side of the tree."

L'Har looked puzzled as she continued, "When I got to the other side of the tree, Timar and Voler were not there. I walked back to the front of the tree, but they were not there either. It is as though they just...vanished."

"Perhaps their path did not go all the way around the tree, but went off in a different direction," Brynn offered.

"I thought of that myself," L'Har said, still looking a bit confused, "so when I went back to the front of the tree I took the left path around, and ended up at the same place I had when I took the right path, on the other side of the tree!"

"I am sure they just went off the path somewhere," Ryu said, standing and brushing the crumbs from his lap. "If you would like, we could help you look for them."

"Ryu," Brynn interrupted, "we really should continue on our path." She looked to the sun in the sky, which was no longer directly overhead, but heading for the horizon. "It is getting late."

"She is right," L'Har said softly as she stood, "you must continue on your path. I will find my way back to my path.

Perhaps Timar and Voler have made their way back to the tree by now. I will go and look for them there."

"But what if they have not?" Paulo asked urgently as he jumped to his feet. "It would not be safe for you to continue The Crossing on your own."

"I will be fine," L'Har answered softly, convincing no one of it.

Ryu thought for a moment before he said, "We will go with you to the tree to look for your friends." Then turning to Brynn he said, "We cannot let her go alone."

Brynn struggled within herself. She knew that Ryu and Paulo were right. L'Har was a small frail girl, and it would not be safe for her to travel by herself. At the same time she could hear her father's voice in her head telling her, *"Do not let anyone or anything distract you from the path,"* which is what he said each time he spoke to her of The Crossing. L'Har looked frightened as she stood waiting for Brynn's answer.

"We will go with you to the tree L'Har," she decided, and stood to go. "If your friends are not there, then you should continue on our path, with us."

L'Har's smile was wide, "Thank you Brynn, that is very kind."

"Will you show us the way?" Ryu asked then.

"Follow me!" L'Har said as she turned back toward the drinking well and the briar bushes beyond. Paulo quickly joined her.

Ryu and Brynn stopped for a moment at the drinking well for some water, and Brynn spoke quietly as she waited for Ryu to finish.

"I do not know why," she said casting a quick glance to make sure L'Har could not hear her, "but there is something about her that makes me uneasy."

Ryu did not understand what she meant. "She is just a small girl Brynn, and she needs our help." L'Har and Paulo were already to the briar bushes. "We should go," he said as he began to walk.

It only took a few moments, and Ryu and Brynn had caught up to the other children. Paulo and L'Har were talking and laughing together as they walked. As they passed the large briar bush that L'Har had been caught in, with its knarled, angry looking branches and prickly thorns, Brynn thought how lucky the girl had been that they had been close enough to hear her cries.

"It was not very lucky that she tripped on a stone and fell into the briar bush in the first place!" she thought to herself.

At that moment something caught Brynn's eye, or rather did not catch her eye. By the base of the big briar bush, where the stone that L'Har said she had tripped over should have been, there was nothing but flat, even dirt. Other than the pile of branches they had broken away to free her, that lay to the side, there was nothing on the ground, nothing at all. Brynn could feel her heart begin to pound, and her chest suddenly felt very heavy. There was no stone.

Chapter 13

Ryu had already caught up to the others, so Brynn kept her suspicions to herself for the moment as she hurried to meet them. "L'Har was lying," Brynn thought to herself, "Ryu and Paulo should know."

L'Har stopped walking then, and she turned to look directly at Brynn. "*You will not tell them!*" Brynn was startled as she clearly heard L'Har's angry words in her head. But with her ears, she could hear the girl saying, "Stop for a moment, we should wait for Brynn to catch up." L'Har's smile was sweet, too sweet, and her eyes were big as they stared directly into Brynn's as she joined them. Brynn felt trapped by her gaze and confused as to what she had or had not heard. She searched Ryu and Paulo's faces to see if they had sensed L'Har's anger, but she saw nothing there. Before she could speak, Ryu broke the moment of silence.

"Which way is it to your path L'Har?" he asked her.

L'Har's stare was broken as she pointed towards the edge of a forest area a hundred or so lengths to the right. "My path goes through those trees," she answered.

The path that they stood on made a long sweeping curve toward the trees up ahead, and entered the forest on the far side. "I cut through the grasses here," L'Har said, pointing to a flattened area beside where they were standing. Ryu could see Brynn's apprehension.

"Ryu, there is something I must tell you…" Brynn started.

"I know Brynn, you are afraid to go through the grasses," Ryu gently interrupted.

"No, that is not..." Brynn protested.

"You should take the path around with Paulo," Ryu continued, ignoring her objection. "I will go through the grasses with L'Har and we can start searching for her friends."

"Yes," said L'Har quickly, "the tree where I lost Voler and Timar is right in the middle. We could all meet there."

"But..." this time it was Paulo who was protesting. He did not want to take the long way with Brynn. He was not afraid of the tall grasses. He wanted to stay with L'Har.

"We are wasting time," L'Har said urgently. "My friends may be hurt."

"We should go," Ryu said and turned to the break in the grasses. "L'Har, you lead the way. Paulo, Brynn, try to hurry." And before either of the other children could protest further, Ryu and L'Har had disappeared into the tall grass.

Paulo was still for a moment, fighting the temptation to follow them. He remembered all too quickly Brynn's fall into the river, and their oath to stay together to make sure everyone was safe. Sighing, he turned and started up the curving path. This time, it was Brynn who followed behind.

"Paulo, wait," Brynn said grabbing his arm. "There is something I must tell you."

There was a note of desperation in her voice that made Paulo stop instantly. "What is wrong Brynn?" he asked, comfortable enough with her now to use her true name in place of her color.

70

"When Ryu and I were behind, catching up with you and L'Har, I stopped to look at the briar bush that she fell into," Brynn started anxiously. "Do you remember that L'Har said that she had tripped on a stone, and fallen?"

Paulo nodded his head. He remembered every word that L'Har had spoken quite clearly.

"There was no stone Paulo." Brynn's eyes grew a little wild as she continued. "And when I started to tell you and Ryu, when I caught up with you, I..." Brynn seemed to search the air for the right words to explain what she had experienced, "...I heard her voice, L'Har's voice, in my head. She was angry and she said not to tell you. About the stone I mean."

Paulo gave her a gentle smile, and Brynn knew instantly that he did not believe her.

"You are tired Brynn, we all are. It is only your mind playing tricks on you." He spoke to her as he would one of the children in his mother's care. "After we help L'Har find her friends, maybe we can stop for a rest. I am sure you will feel much better." Paulo turned to go.

"Paulo please, listen to me!" Brynn said grabbing his arm again.

"No," Paulo said curtly, "Ryu said we must try to hurry. L'Har needs our help. We have to go now." And before Brynn could say another word, Paulo turned away and started to run up the path toward the trees.

"Why will he not listen?!" Brynn said out loud, frustrated, as she started after him.

Brynn could feel a heavy feeling settle into the pit of her stomach as she hurried to follow Paulo, who was running as fast as his legs would carry him.

"Trust yourself Brynn." It was her father's voice again in her head. He had said those words to her many times in the past. Whenever she was unsure, or afraid, or asked him what the right thing to do was, he would always tell her *"Trust yourself. Your head, heart and instinct will always help make things clear."*

Just then, the words of the second riddle came to her mind:

> *You must choose what to believe*
> *Your eyes and ears, they can deceive*
> *You can not win.*

"I believe L'Har is a not telling the truth," Brynn said angrily to herself as she made her way around the curve of the path. Paulo was almost to the entrance of the forest. "I do not think she is at all what she seems."

> *You can not win.*

Those words echoed in her mind just as she caught up Paulo, who had stopped to let his eyes adjust to the darkness of the forest.

"There she is! There is L'Har!" Paulo exclaimed, pointing to her up ahead.

Brynn squeezed her eyes tight, and when she opened them, she could see the little girl a few hundred lengths away. The path sloped down somewhat, and stopped right at the base of a very large, very old looking tree that was bordered on both sides by very dense brush. L'Har stood beside it, waving to them.

"Come on!" Paulo said excitedly, but was careful as he hurried down the incline.

"Yes, there she is," Brynn said to herself, studying the girl for a moment before she started to make her way down the path.

You can not win.

Was that L'Har's voice in her head? Brynn froze, and in spite of the distance between them, she could see the look of contempt on L'Har's face.

Suddenly an enormous wave of fear swept over her, as she realized something was wrong, very wrong. L'Har was there, but where was Ryu? Brynn looked everywhere but she could not see him, only the big old tree, with the tangled brush on either side of it and L'Har standing on the path.

L'Har was grinning as she watched Paulo make his way down to her. The fear gripped Brynn even tighter. Where was Ryu? Paulo had made it down the slope and was now standing with L'Har. A sense of panic overtook her and Brynn started to run toward them. She shouted out desperately as she ran, "Where is Ryu?!"

Chapter 14

Brynn could see L'Har whispering to Paulo as she ran toward them. The panic rose in her as she willed herself to run faster. Paulo was smiling as L'Har took his hand, and without even a glance toward Brynn, they started up the path to the left of the large old tree.

"No! Paulo wait!" Brynn called out frantically. She was still a hundred lengths or so away. Paulo was not listening as L'Har led him into the brush beside the tree and out of sight. "Paulo, stop!"

You can not win.

This time Brynn was sure it was L'Har's voice in her head, using the words to mock her. Brynn stopped when she reached the old tree.

"Paulo?" she called out. "Ryu?" There was only silence. "Paulo, Ryu, where are you?" Again, there was no answer. "Ryu?" she called once more.

Tittering laughter floated through the air. Fear swelled in Brynn's chest. L'Har appeared out of the brush, giggling and skipping along with light, graceful steps. She stopped and her laughter faded as she saw Brynn.

"Where is Paulo?" Brynn asked anxiously. "Where is Ryu?"

L'Har's smile was forced, her words seemed dipped in sarcasm, "They are on the other side of the tree looking for Timar and Voler of course." She took a few steps toward

Brynn, and her smile grew bigger. "They sent me back to wait for you, Brynn."

Sensing danger, Brynn shouted, "Stop!" as she held up her hands. "Do not come any closer."

L'Har continued to move toward her, her smile turning dark. "You do not need to be afraid, Brynn. Just come with me and everything will be alright."

"I do not believe you!" Brynn said, as she backed away from the small, pretty girl, whose face suddenly looked years older than it had only a moment ago. "What have you done with Paulo and Ryu? What have you done with my friends?"

L'Har stopped walking and her expression was serious. "Your friends?" she asked venomously, "Your friends? You think Paulo and Ryu are your friends?"

"I know they are my friends, L'Har," Brynn said defiantly. "What have you done with them?"

"Really? They are your friends?" L'Har spat the words at her. "If they are your friends, why did they leave you behind?"

"Ryu hurried to help you find your friends," Brynn answered indignantly. "Although there are no friends, are there?"

L'Har ignored her question. "But Ryu left both you and Paulo behind, did he not? The three of you swore you would stay together, after you fell into the river, did you not?"

"How did you..?" Brynn mumbled, confused.

"Even though he could have waited until you reached us,
Paulo chose to follow the path with me," L'Har continued.
"He did not want to wait for you, he wanted to find Ryu.
His "best friend" is what Paulo called him."

L'Har moved toward Brynn until she was standing only a
length away. "He wanted to stay with me, not you!"
L'Har's face was twisted in anger now. "You see Brynn,
they are not really your friends, they only stay with you
because they think you can not take care of yourself."

"Ryu knows I can..." Brynn started, but then stopped
herself. Somehow she knew that anger was exactly what
this girl wanted from her. She would not give in to it.
Brynn forced herself to be calm, and stared right into the
eyes of the angelic looking stranger she knew was anything
but innocent.

"I do not believe you L'Har. I do not believe anything you
say," Brynn said firmly and started to walk toward her. The
girl began to back away slowly. "I know you lied about
falling into the bush. There was no rock. I know you lied
about losing your friends."

L'Har stumbled as she tripped over a rocked on the path.
"Yes, yes I did," she stammered. "I mean, yes, I did lose
my friends."

"No, L'Har, you did not," Brynn said firmly as she
continued to walk toward her. "And somehow you
bewitched both Ryu and Paulo. You made them follow
you."

"They wanted to leave you. They said you were slowing them down. They told me, they both told me." L'Har almost fell as she backed into the old tree. Steadying herself, she stood and brushing the hair from her face, she looked at Brynn with unbridled hatred. "They only pretended to be your friends."

Brynn stopped and stared at the girl who had seemed so helpless, the pretty waif that Ryu was so quick to help and Paulo was so eager to follow. She realized that she was not at all what she appeared to be. Brynn would not listen to one more word.

"You are a liar L'Har."

"No!" L'Har called out, her eyes turning from crystal blue to the darkest black. A wind surrounded her suddenly, whipping her hair and dress in its circular whirl. Brynn had to shield her eyes as leaves and dirt flew everywhere. The wind grew faster and stronger, and Brynn could no longer see L'Har in the funnel of flying debris.

It was over in an instant. The wind tunnel was gone and it had taken the little girl it had trapped with it. Brynn's ears adjusted to the silence as she watched the last of the leaves flutter to the forest floor. A sense of relief washed over her.

"I did win!" she thought triumphantly. Her elation was quickly overshadowed by the panic she had felt earlier. She had to find her friends.

Brynn stared at the giant tree trunk before her. Both the path on the left and the path on the right seemed equally dark and foreboding. She knew that L'Har had taken Paulo down the path to the left, but she did not know where it led.

"Ryu? Paulo?" she called out hopefully, "Can you hear me?" There was only quiet. "Ryu, Paulo, where are you?" she shouted again, as loud as she could.

"Brynn? Brynn is that you?" Brynn strained to hear the words, which were very faint and seemed to be coming from very far away. It was Ryu.

"Yes Ryu, it is me," Brynn shouted back in answer. Tears of relief gathered in her eyes, "Are you alright? Where are you? Is Paulo with you?"

"Yes, he is here. We are not hurt. We are in the tree."

Brynn looked up into the tree's huge canopy of branches and leaves. She could not see either Ryu or Paulo. "Where in the tree? Are you high up in the branches?"

"No Brynn," Ryu answered. She had to listen hard, as she was still barely able to hear his words. "We are not up in the branches. I am not sure how we got here, but we are inside the tree. We are inside the trunk itself."

Chapter 15

Brynn pressed her hands against the dry, rough bark of the giant tree. Its trunk was as thick as ten of the old oak trees back in the village. "Inside the tree? But how?" she shouted. "Is there a way in?"

"I...do not know." Pressing her ear to the trunk of the tree, Brynn could hear Ryu's words more clearly. She could also hear the confusion and fear in his voice.

"I will go around to the other side, there must be an opening there," Brynn shouted.

"No!" Ryu yelled back. "It was when we followed L'Har around the tree that we ended up here. Please do not go to the other side Brynn, it is not safe."

"But how will you get out?" she asked. For this, Ryu had no answer.

"It is very dark," Ryu yelled, "but we will try our best to look around us."

"I will find a way. I will find a way to get you out," Brynn assured him and began to search every square inch of the trunk with her hands. There was not even a knot in the bark. She got down on her hands and knees, to see if there was a space under the roots where she might squeeze through, but the roots held tight to the dirt. She could see no opening anywhere. "I will have to cut through the tree," Brynn thought to herself and set about finding a sharp rock to begin the enormous task.

Just then a loud chirping rang through the forest. It was an urgent sound, like an alarm of sorts, and Brynn stopped her search to look where it was coming from.

Flying toward her was a bird, the same small brown kind that had led them on the path away from the river earlier that afternoon. "Is this the same bird that helped us before?" she thought to herself. The bird stopped and hovered a length away. And, as though it could hear her thoughts, the little bird nodded his head.

"Have you come to help me?" Brynn asked sheepishly.

The bird nodded again, turned, and flew toward the bushes to right of the large tree. It fluttered back and forth in front of the wall of leaves and branches. It seemed to be looking for something. A few moments later it stopped, turned and chirped three times. Brynn understood that the bird meant for her to come to where it was. She made her way up the path and looked at the dense growth that the bird was motioning to. She could see no opening.

"I do not understand. There is no path into the bushes," Brynn said, bewildered.

The little brown bird trilled again three times, turned and flew slowly toward the branches. In an instant it disappeared. It was though it had just...vanished.

Brynn could hardly believe her eyes.

"How...?"

And then the bird was back, appearing right where it had hovered moments earlier. It chirped again, this time only once.

"Is it some sort of magic?" Brynn asked in amazement. The bird chirped once, as if to answer, "Yes". Then it turned and disappeared once again.

Taking a deep breath, Brynn started after the bird. "I sure hope it knows what it is doing," she muttered, moving very slowly, arms extended out in front of her. She shut her eyes tight.

Brynn felt the air turn cold around her and her stomach jumped like she was falling, yet she could feel the ground beneath her feet. Her hands felt as though they were pushing through water, although they did not feel wet. She shivered as the rest of her body passed through the vortex, but it was only a moment later when she felt the sunlight on her skin.

As the little bird chirped its loud alarm once again, Brynn stopped walking and opened her eyes. She could see she was standing a few lengths away from the entrance of what looked to be a tunnel into the tree.

"Are my friends in there?" she asked the bird. Once again it nodded its head in answer. The little brown bird flew to the mouth of the tunnel, turned and hovered, waiting for Brynn to follow.

As she started to walk, Brynn's eyes were drawn to something shiny in the dirt just in front of the tree. Bending down, she could see that it was flat and smooth, and not just one color, but many. "A Legacy Stone!" she cried out as she hurried to pick it up. She marveled at its beauty as she cleaned the dirt away and held it up to the light.

Brynn was not thinking of its significance at that moment however, but wishing for the same light that Ryu's Legacy Stone had given him. She could see nothing but black as she looked into the tunnel. Sighing, she placed the stone in the pouch fastened to her waist and approached the entrance. The little brown bird chirped once and then once again, hovered for a moment longer and then flew away.

"No!" Brynn cried after it, "Please do not leave! I need you."

"Trust yourself, Brynn. You will be fine." It was her father's voice in her head again, and she felt her heart long for him now. He had always told her that she was smart and strong and brave, and that she could do anything she set her mind to. She held on to those words as she took a deep breath and started forward.

Brynn felt swallowed by the darkness as she took her first few cautious steps. She felt the dirt beneath her feet sloping downward, and mindful of her fall into the river, inched her way down. She could hear something that sounded like the scraping of the trees against the windows of her cottage back home when The Winds came.

"Ryu? Paulo?" she called out as the fear started to rise in her ,"Can you hear me?" She heard only silence.

"Ryu?" she called out as loud as she could, "Are you there?"

"Yes, we are here!" Ryu called back. His words still seemed very far away, and now Brynn could tell that they were coming from down below. "Where are you?"
"There is a tunnel down to where you are, I am coming!" Brynn shouted.

"A tunnel?" Ryu yelled back. "But we have found no…"

Brynn did not hear the rest of Ryu's words. At that moment she felt someone, or something, push her hard from behind. She stumbled forward first one step, then another. When she went to put her foot down the third time, there was no ground beneath it. She cried out in surprise. And even though she was surrounded by black, Brynn squeezed her eyes tight as she fell.

Chapter 16

It was a dozen lengths before she hit the hard dirt. Brynn whimpered as she heard the bones in her arm crack. She had landed on a ledge at the top of a steep incline, but the force of the fall propelled her over the edge and she rolled down quickly. Brynn did her best to shield her injured arm as she tumbled over and over and over.

Finally the slope ended, and luckily it was Brynn's feet that met the large boulder at the bottom. Brynn lay for a moment catching her breath before she sat up and looked around her, wincing as she cradled her broken left arm with her right one. It was pitch black, and she could see nothing.

"Ryu?" she called out, "Can you hear me?"

"Yes, Brynn! We are right here!" Ryu's voice came from the other side of the rock, only a few lengths away. In Brynn's pouch, The Legacy Stone began to glow. Carefully Brynn reached in, brought out the stone, and held it up over her head.

"Can you see the light?" she asked as she tried to stand, her broken arm making it awkward to do so.

"A Legacy Stone!" Paulo gasped. They were the first words he had spoken since finding himself in the tree. Ryu had mistaken his silence for fear, when in reality Paulo had been silent out of shame. He was ashamed at how easily he had been misled by L'Har. He was ashamed that he had left Brynn alone on the path in the forest. But mostly he was ashamed at how easy it was for the pretty little girl to charm him.

"Yes!" cried Ryu, "We see it!"

Now with the help of the light, Ryu could see that what his hands had felt as another large tree root was in fact a tall stalagmite poking up from the dirt. There was a gap a half a length wide on one side where the light from Brynn's Legacy Stone shone through.

The boys were only a few lengths away, and it was only moments before they squeezed through the gap and found Brynn on the other side. Paulo threw his arms around I her and began to sob. "I am…so…sorry!" he cried.

Brynn gasped in pain as he bumped against her injured arm, dropping the Legacy Stone.

"You are hurt!" Ryu exclaimed as he gently pulled Paulo back and bent to pick up the stone.

Brynn nodded, fighting back the tears, "Yes. I think I may have broken my arm." She motioned to the incline behind her. "It is very steep. I fell and then rolled a long way."

Ryu placed the Legacy Stone in Brynn's pouch and ripped a wide strip of cloth from the bottom of his tunic. He made a sling for Brynn's broken arm, as he had seen his mother do many times. He was careful as he tied the knot on her shoulder, "This will keep it steady, and should help with the pain."

"Thank you Ryu," Brynn said quietly. She was grateful for his help and thankful to have found him. The tears in her eyes were now tears of relief.

"We will have to crawl up," Ryu said, looking towards the incline. "Paulo and I will help you, Brynn."

Paulo quickly nodded, "I will never leave you again Brynn!" he promised, as guilt washed over him once more.

Brynn gave him a warm smile as she brushed away a tear that had rolled down his cheek. "I know Paulo," she said softly. "I know."

Through the fabric of Brynn's pouch, the light from The Legacy Stone showed that the tunnel she had rolled through was only a few lengths wide. Slowly, the three made their way up on their hands and knees through the loose dirt that covered the incredibly sharp angle of the hill. A few times it gave way under them, and they fell back a few lengths. It seemed a long time passed before they could finally see rays of sunlight.

It took all of their energy to reach the top of the slope, and Ryu, using a vine that was hanging from the edge of the ledge, hoisted himself up to the top. Paulo helped lift Brynn as Ryu pulled her with the vine and then climbed up himself. By the time they reached the mouth of the cave, all three were drenched in sweat and gasping for breath.

When he could finally speak, Ryu turned to Brynn. "Thank you," he said, his voice choked with emotion, "Thank you for finding us."

Brynn just nodded as she was over whelmed thinking of all that had happened and struggling against the pain from her broken arm.

Fear gripped Paulo. He jumped up and moved quickly to stand close to his friends. "Where is L'Har?" he asked, his eyes wide as they searched the surrounding brush.

"It is alright Paulo. She is gone," Brynn said as she tried to stand, her arm making it difficult to push herself up.

Ryu stood, took her by her good arm, and lifted her to her feet. He turned his attention to the crude sling he had made, trying to make it more comfortable. She winced slightly as she continued, "She was not real. When I asked where you both had gone, she said you had left me. She told me that you and Ryu were not my friends, that you only stayed with me because you felt sorry for me. I told her she was a liar. She grew angry and changed into a frightening looking spirit. A twirling wind came and took her away."

Paulo's mouth was agape as he listened. And then guilt entered his heart once again. "She led me beside the tree," he said as he remembered running away from Brynn when he had seen L'Har in the forest. "She told me to lay my hand on the bark, saying that it was a 'singing' tree, and that I could feel the vibrations if I touched it." Once again his eyes filled with tears. "The next thing I knew I was in the darkness with Ryu."

"She said the same to me," Ryu said quietly and met his young friend's eyes, "I too was fooled."

"She fooled us all," Brynn said, reaching out to take Paulo's hand in hers and giving Ryu a small smile.

The sound of running water interrupted their thoughts just then.

"Do you hear that?" Ryu asked, "It sounds like a stream." Aching with thirst, the friends started toward the direction the sound was coming from.

They found themselves on another path the wound through the thick trees. A short distance away, they came upon a large clearing, about a hundred or so lengths in each direction, filled with beautiful flowers of every color imaginable. Next to it was a small stream that flowed quickly with crystal clear water. They all quickly knelt at the bank and used their hands to drink.

Her injured arm making it difficult to hold her balance, Brynn rose and walked a few lengths upstream to where a large rock sat on the bank, thinking it would be a good place to steady herself. As she approached it, she could see the large letters etched deeply into its surface. Her heart pounded with a mixture of excitement and dread. The words of the last riddle entered her mind.

> *You must choose what to believe*
> *Your eyes and ears, they can deceive*
> *You can not win.*

Brynn realized then that the last riddle had been a warning. It had been a warning as to the danger that they would encounter. It was a warning about L'Har, one which none of them had heeded.

Chapter 17

With reluctance, Brynn called out to Ryu and Paulo, "I have found another riddle." The boys hurried to where she stood.

Lessons learned will help you know
It will bloom again like the flowers that grow
It is simple

"Simple?" Paulo said to his friends, frustrated. "Nothing has been simple."

Ryu and Brynn only stared at the words before them, both thinking of all that they had been through thus far. To them it was also very difficult to imagine any part of this journey as being simple or easy.

"Rakkaus! Rakkaus, where are you?!" The voice came from the far end of the clearing. Looking they could see an elderly woman carrying something in her hand walking slowly in their direction. "Rakkaus, you silly boy, I have brought your favorite treat!" They all watched her for a moment. She seemed to be searching for something amongst the flowers.

It was Ryu who called out, "Excuse me, have you lost something?"

The old woman looked up from her task in surprise. "Oh, hello. I did not see you children there," she called back.

"My name is Ryu," he introduced himself, "These are my friends Brynn and Paulo."

"Hello," Brynn called to her and gave a small wave.

Paulo could feel panic over take him. "Ryu!" he thought to himself angrily, "We are not permitted to use our true names!" A feeling of foreboding had come over him when he looked at the old woman. As his two friends started to walk toward her, he hesitated a few moments before following.

"Why hello there!" the old woman said with a large warm smile. "I am Duvera. I live in a cottage just beyond this clearing." Noticing Brynn's sling, she asked, "Are you hurt?"

Brynn's cheeks flushed a bright red, "I am fine, really. I just fell on my arm." Duvera started to question her more, but Brynn was quick to ask, "Have you lost something?"

"Yes, Brynn," Duvera said distracted, placing the small wooden cage she had been carrying down in the dirt beside her. "My pet mouse, Rakkaus has wandered away from our home again. We are each other's only company and I think every once in a while he tires of my constant chatter and wanders out to find peace and quiet!" Duvera smiled then, and her smile reminded Ryu of his grandmother's, a very wise, kind woman.

Duvera was quite small and feeble looking, with long grey hair tied in a braid that reached nearly to her feet. She wore a simple dress of pale blue with sturdy walking shoes. At her waist was a thick belt with many small pouches hanging from it. Her deep set brown eyes had seen many seasons come and go.

"We will help you look," Ryu offered.

"Oh, that would be very kind, very kind indeed," Duvera said with relief, as she rested her hand on his arm. "My eyes do not work as well as they used to!"

"What does he look like, your mouse?" Brynn asked, her eyes already scanning the flower bed.

"He is a light brown, Brynn," Duvera answered, "with a little pink nose and a long pink tail. Here," she said reaching into one of the pouches tied to her waist, "I have brought Rakkaus' favorite treat, small pieces of carrots." She handed a few to each of the children. "He will come to you if you offer him these."

Ryu and Brynn set about looking for the mouse. Ryu headed toward the trees at the entrance to the clearing, thinking that the mouse might be looking for food on the forest floor. Brynn cradled her injured arm as she bent over to look down into the flower bed for Rakkaus. Paulo however paid more attention to Duvera than to searching for her pet. He still could not shake his uneasy feeling as he watched her moving slowly through the flowers, calling to Rakkaus.

Without realizing it, Paulo had wandered back toward the rock by the stream where Brynn had found the riddle. His eyes were drawn to its words.

Lessons learned will help you know
It will bloom again like the flowers that grow
It is simple

"I have learned that things are not always what they seem," Paulo said to himself, ashamed, remembering yet again how easy it had been for L'Har to trick him.

He looked to Duvera, who appeared to be a harmless old woman, and felt a mixture of fear and alarm in the pit of his stomach. Before he had a chance to consider her further, he heard a small squeak. Sitting no more than half a length in front of him, on the bank of the stream, was a little brown mouse. It just sat and stared at him, its little pink nose twitching as though smelling for danger.

Paulo's demeanor softened. "Hello Rakkaus," he said, kneeling down ever so slowly as to not scare the little mouse away. He reached out his arm and opened his hand to show him the pieces of carrot, "I have a treat for you."

Rakkaus seemed to consider him a moment before rushing forward to see what he held. As the small mouse crept towards his hand to claim his prize, Paulo scooped him up gently. Standing, he called out to the others. "I have found him!"

Duvera rushed, as best she could, to where Paulo stood. "Rakkaus, there you are!" she said with an enormous sigh of relief.

Opening the door to the small cage, she motioned for Paulo to put him in. "I can not thank you enough Paulo," Duvera said meeting his eyes with a gentle smile. "I do not know what I would do without my only friend."

Instantly Paulo's feelings of dread were replaced with pity at her words. How lonely Duvera must be out here all alone with only a brown mouse for a friend he thought.

"One good friend is all you need," Duvera said as she latched the gate of the cage. Smiling, she drew the rest of the carrot treats out of her pouch and put them in the cage for Rakkaus to eat.

Paulo froze for a moment. How had she known what he was thinking? Who, or what, was this little old lady who stood before him. She met his anxious stare with a gentle smile.

Ryu and Brynn joined them then. "Thank you all for helping me search," Duvera said kindly. She studied the three children, whose clothes were streaked with dirt, leaves and twigs tangled in their hair. "You three look as though you could use a snack. May I offer you some tea and cookies before you continue on your way? My cottage is only a short way away."

"No!" Paulo blurted out, his fears taking over. "The sun is moving quickly to the horizon, we must be on our way!"

"Paulo," Brynn replied, surprised by his outburst, "Do not be rude." Turning to Duvera she politely accepted the old woman's invitation, "We would be glad to have afternoon tea with you."

"Yes," said Ryu, sensing the old woman's eagerness for their company, "Thank you for your generous offer." He knew that he and his friends could use a much needed rest before continuing on the path of The Crossing.

"Lovely," Duvera said as she turned back up the path. "Follow me this way."

Ryu and Brynn followed close behind in the old woman's slow deliberate steps. Paulo did not move. He could not shake the feeling of danger that had a tight grip on him.

Ryu stopped, turning to look over his shoulder. He saw Paulo, still standing by The Riddle rock, as still and expressionless as a statue. Ryu was puzzled as to why his friend was not following. "Paulo," he called out to him, "We must go. Hurry."

Chapter 18

Paulo did not hurry. Instead he walked quite slowly as he fought the urge to call out to his friends, to tell them that they should not go with Duvera. Part of him, the part that was weary and hungry, welcomed the thought of a nice warm cup of tea and some sweets. The other part could not help but fear that they were walking into another trap.

On the other side of the clearing, just inside the entrance to the forest, was a smaller path that led into the trees to the left. A few dozen lengths down it sat a quaint little cottage made of large stones. A small stream of smoke rose from the chimney stack poking out of its thatched roof. Duvera paused for a moment at the entrance, waiting patiently for Paulo to join them. As she pulled open the large wooden door and motioned the children in, they were enveloped by the enticing smell of fresh baking.

"I had just finished a batch of honey-nut cookies before I went looking for Rakkaus," Duvera said as she hung the cage that held the little brown mouse on a hook that was on the wall near the window. She motioned to a long stone table that sat near the hearth and its low burning fire, "Please sit."

Paulo was quick to study his surroundings as Duvera busied herself at the stove preparing tea. The cottage was small, with sparse furnishings. It was quite neat and orderly, with not much in the way of decoration. Only a small framed drawing of a tree, one very similar to the old oak by the pond in their village, hung on the wall over the mantle. It looked to have been drawn by a child.

"I know you must still have a long journey ahead of you," Duvera said as she laid out a large plate of cookies, "But rest for a moment now. You will need your strength." She brought them cups, and it was only a few moments before the kettle whistled and she poured the tea.

The children ate and drank in silence, considering her words. *"You will need your strength."* Paulo wondered if they were some sort warning. The hairs at the base of his neck refused to lie down.

Ryu forced himself to sit tall. All that had happened had drained not only his strength, but had left him with little courage as well.

Brynn knew that her broken arm would make the rest of the journey more difficult and wondered if what little strength she had left would be enough. Duvera could see that they were all lost in their own thoughts and moved silently as she tidied the baking dishes.

"Do you live here alone?" asked Ryu finally as he finished the last of his tea.

"Yes," Duvera answered, joining them at the table then with a cup of tea for herself. "My husband passed to The Great Beyond almost six seasons ago."

Paulo's eyes moved back to the drawing on the wall. He asked, "Do you have any children?"

"We had a daughter," Duvera answered with a small smile. Paulo could see the sadness in her eyes as she followed his gaze to the drawing on the wall. "She too is gone. But that was a very long time ago."

Sensing her pain, the children dared not ask what had happened. Duvera pulled open the string of a pouch fastened to her belt at the very front. She took out a small hair ribbon that perhaps at one time had been white, but had long since yellowed with age. She ran her fingers along the smoothness of it as she continued.

"She was lost during The Crossing," Duvera said quietly, as she looked away from them, her eyes filling with tears.

Brynn gasped. "What happened?", she could not help asking.

Duvera rose and walked to the picture on the wall, "It was near the end of the journey. The sun was only a speck on the horizon, and the moon was rising quickly in the sky. The others that were with her, Bolond and Haastig, took a short cut through tall grasses to make it to the village before dark. Aina, my daughter, refused to leave the safety of the path and would not follow them."

Duvera's eyes clouded over as she remembered, "We waited only a short while before a group of men from our village went out to look for her." She turned and a single tear rolled down her cheek. "They could not find her."

The silence that followed was filled with her sorrow. Ryu, Brynn and Paulo could find no words to offer comfort, as their minds were filled full of the possible perils the young girl had encountered.

Duvera's voice was still soft as she wiped away the tear. "My husband, Sabio, searched for days, from sun up and into the night. Soon after, he built this cottage close to where the others had seen her last, hoping that she would find her way back to us."

Turning and seeing the anguish on the three children's faces, Duvera was brought back to the present. "I am so sorry children, I did not mean to frighten you."

Brynn managed to utter a polite, "I am very sorry for your loss," feeling very sorry indeed for this lonely old woman who had shown them such kindness.

Duvera gave her a warm smile, "Thank you Brynn, that is very thoughtful."

She rejoined them at the table and began clearing away the dishes. "The Crossing is a very difficult journey for every child. I can see by Brynn's injury alone that you have already encountered dangers along its path."

Ryu, Brynn and Paulo just nodded, remembering every moment of their journey thus far. Each struggled to understand all that had happened, and they each struggled even more so with the guilt of their actions.

"I fell into the river," Brynn said, her voice low, remembering how stubborn she had been, wanting to travel the path of The Crossing alone. "I would have surely died had Ryu and Paulo not saved me."

"I left my friends and put them in danger," Ryu admitted quickly, racked with guilt as he remembered how saving L'Har's friends had been more important to him at that moment than looking after his own.

"Had I not deserted Brynn, she would not have been hurt," Paulo said, his eyes cast downward in shame, remembering how trying to please L'Har had made him forget his pledge to protect his friend.

"Do not fret children," Duvera said soothingly as she lowered herself onto the bench beside Ryu once again. "I can see that the bond of friendship between you is strong."

She met each child's eyes intently then. "Over the years, living here in this cottage, I have met many children on the journey of The Crossing. I have heard many stories of The Nothings and The Somethings they have encountered and each child tells a different tale. There are those that will try to deceive you and those that will try to help you."

Sighing, Duvera continued. "I cannot tell you what may or may not happen on your journey, and I have only one piece of advice to offer." The children listened intently to her words.

"No matter who or what you may happen upon, no matter what manner of trickery or magic you face, you must always remember this: the three of you are much stronger together than you could ever be alone."

Chapter 19

As they stood in the doorway of the little cottage, the children thanked Duvera for her kindness. They had only a short time now before the sun would meet the horizon, and they knew that they must go.

"Here," Duvera said, handing a small satchel to Paulo. "I have packed a few more cookies and a flask of water should you need another rest before you get home to your village."

Paulo felt a tug at his heart and impulsively he wrapped his arms around Duvera in a warm embrace. "Thank you," he said softly as he rested his head on her shoulder, "for everything." Not wanting to leave the safety and comfort that he felt, it was a few moments before he forced himself to let go.

Duvera ruffled Paulo's hair with a smile, just as his father had always done, and Paulo instantly felt an intense longing to be back with him now. "Now boys, you will have to look out for Brynn," she advised. "I can see by the way her arm hangs that the bone is most likely broken, and she will need you both to help her where the path becomes difficult."

"Difficult," Paulo thought to himself, and the words of the riddle by the stream came rushing back in his mind.

Lessons learned will help you know
It will bloom again like the flowers that grow
It is simple

A grin spread across his face as Paulo remembered how he had felt when he first saw Duvera and how he felt looking at her now. He had his answer to the riddle.

Just then, the Legacy Stone in Brynn's pouch began to glow brightly.

"A Legacy Stone!" Duvera exclaimed clapping her hands together, "I knew you were a Champion Brynn!"

Favoring her bad arm, Brynn gingerly reached into her pouch and took out the stone, its light shining as bright as a twinkling star in the sky.

"Here," Duvera said excitedly, reaching to take it from her hand, "I believe I may know what it is telling you to do." Carefully, she placed the Legacy Stone on the palm of Brynn's hand in the sling. The white light from the stone grew even brighter, and seemed to travel up Brynn's arm to her shoulder.

Paulo and Ryu stood watching, mouths agape as Brynn's fingers closed into a fist. There was one last burst of intense light from between Brynn's fingers and when she opened them, the stone was gone.

"It is healed!", Brynn said with a gasp. "The Legacy Stone has healed my arm." Removing the sling from around her neck, she straightened and then bent her arm. Other than a lingering stiffness, her arm was indeed totally healed.

"How did you know? How did you know it would heal her?" Ryu asked Duvera, amazed at what he had seen.

"My Sabio," Duvera answered with a smile, her brown eyes shining brightly. "Ages ago, when he had made the journey of The Crossing, he too found a Legacy Stone. He had fallen into a deep hole and twisted his ankle quite badly. He had placed the stone into his boot for safe keeping earlier. His Legacy Stone had healed his injury. I somehow knew Brynn's Legacy Stone meant to do the same."

This time it was Brynn who reached out to hug the slight old woman tightly, "Thank you Duvera. I will never forget all you have done."

It was many moments before she too had to force herself to end the embrace as Paulo had to, her heart filled with both gratitude.

The boys said one last good-bye and then headed up the path away from the cottage toward the forest.

Brynn hesitated a moment before following. "Would it be alright if I came to visit you here now and again?" she asked quietly. "That is after we finish The Crossing, of course."

Her eyes soft as she looked at the beautiful, brave girl before her, Duvera answered, "Yes Brynn, I would like that very much." She did not have the heart to tell her that she knew they would never see each other again.

A few children over the years had promised the same, to visit Duvera again once their Crossing was over. But the old woman knew that the one truth of The Crossing, that its path was ever changing, would prevent Brynn from ever finding her cottage again.

With a final wave to Duvera, Brynn hurried after her friends. When she joined them, the three stood together at the entrance to the forest.

"Which way do we go?" Brynn asked, having lost her bearings after all that had happened.

"The sun is moving that way," Paulo said, pointing to the sky over the trees ahead of them. "We should go back and follow the stream."

"Yes," said Ryu with certainty, both his spirit and courage re-ignited by the thought of seeing his family again. "The stream by the clearing must lead toward our village."

They turned back to where they had first met Duvera, and came to the green banks by the water.

"It is still a long way. We have yet to cross over The Foothills. We must move quickly if we are to make it to the village before dark," Ryu said and started to run, mindful to keep his pace to where Paulo could keep up. Brynn kept in stride beside the younger boy to make sure she did not get ahead.

The stream widened slightly as they went, its waters turned from clear to dark, and they could no longer see the bed of rocks it flowed over. The children ran for quite a while along the bank, parallel to the forest, the warm rays of the late afternoon sun shining down upon them.

Suddenly, the waters of the stream seemed to make a sharp turn in front of them, away from the path the sun was taking across the sky. The children stopped, considering what to do next.

"We must cross the stream," Brynn said, her breathing heavy from running.

"It is not very wide," Ryu said, wiping the beads of sweat from his forehead with the arm of his tunic, "but we could not jump across."

"We will have to swim," Paulo said when he finally caught his breath, "or make a bridge."

"We do not know if there are dangers in the water," Brynn said hurriedly, still fearful after her fall into the river.

"Yes, there could be Sliver Fish", Paulo agreed, searching the waters with his eyes as he remembered then the time he had gone wading in The Red Mud Stream back home with his sister Pia and brother Piero.

Pia had wandered into a school of Sliver Fish, and her legs had been cut quite badly. It had been many days before her wounds had healed.

"Then we must find a log or a large branch and make a bridge," Ryu said as he walked towards the edge of the forest. Brynn followed closely behind.

As Paulo turned to follow, something in the stream a few lengths ahead caught his eye. He stopped for a moment, but could see nothing but the calm dark water.

Thinking that his imagination was getting the best of him, he shook his head and went to follow Ryu and Brynn, but then his eyes saw movement in the water once again.

This time Paulo stopped and watched for a few moments longer. A very large fish, bright yellow like the new bud on the branch of an Ever Flower Tree, jumped out of the stream and seemed to hover before continuing its arch back into the water. A moment later, a dazzling orange fish, the same type as the one before, jumped in the same place, in the same way as the one before it had. A moment after that came a bright red fish. Then a royal purple, brilliant blue and ever green fish, all one moment apart, jumping in a slow arch out of the stream where Paulo had seen the first.

For a few moments, there was no movement, and then the first yellow fish appeared out of the water again. This time as it hovered, Paulo could hear clearly the word the fish spoke in his head.

"We," the yellow fish said, and disappeared into the water.

Then the orange fish appeared. "Will", said its voice in Paulo's mind.

"Show," was the word from the red fish as it jumped.

"You," said the purple one.

"The," said the brilliant blue fish.

And finally, from the green fish - "Way," it said before diving into the dark water of the stream.

Chapter 20

Scarcely believing his own eyes, Paulo watched as the fish continued to jump in the same pattern a third time. Again, Paulo heard the words of the brightly colored fish clearly in his mind.

"We. Will. Show. You. The. Way."

Struggling to find his voice, Paulo called out to his friends, who were searching just at the edge of the trees for something to help them cross the stream. "Ryu, Brynn, come quick! You must see this!"

The tone of Paulo's voice made Ryu and Brynn run to him immediately.

"What is it Paulo? Are you alright?" Brynn asked, concerned as she joined him on the bank of the stream.

As Ryu came to them, he could see the look of amazement on his young friend's face.

"Look, there," Paulo said, pointing to the water where he had first seen the yellow fish. Only now, there was nothing to see but the calm dark water.

"What is it you are trying to show us Paulo?" Ryu asked, confused. He could see nothing but water where Paulo was pointing.

"Wait, just wait," Paulo said excitedly.

And sure enough, a few moments later, the yellow fish poked its head out of the water, and jumped high in the air.

"We," It said again, only this time both Ryu and Brynn could hear the word in their head as well. And once more, the rainbow of fish; orange, red, purple, blue and green made their arc out of the water, and each said the same words Paulo had heard before.

"Will. Show. You. The. Way."

Brynn stared at the water, astonished.

"How?" asked Ryu, moving closer to where the fish were jumping. "How will you show us the way?"

In answer, the fish began their series of jumps, only this time they jumped much faster, and their words seemed more urgent.

"We. Will. Show. You. The. Way."

Ryu stood on the bank of the stream directly where the fish were appearing and stared into the water. The yellow fish appeared once more, and this time when it jumped the children heard a different word in their minds.

"Here," it said.

All the commotion had stirred up the water quite a bit, and suddenly Ryu could see that in front of him, just below the surface of the water were large flat stones, less than a length apart, that made a path to the bank on the other side. When the water was calm, they would be nearly impossible to see, but the motion of the fish had made them visible.

"A path!' Ryu exclaimed, "There is a path of stones in the water!"

Paulo and Brynn came to where he was, and they too saw the stones.

"We can cross here!" Paulo said with a grin.

Looking down, he could see that the six fish were swimming in circles under the water, three on each side of the stones. "Thank you," he said to them, "Thank you for showing us the way."

He remembered then the cookies in the satchel Duvera had given him, reached in and pulled out three of them. Keeping one, he handed one to each of his friends. The children crumbled the cookies up into smaller pieces and scattered them in the water. The fish ate hungrily, and once they were done, disappeared into the dark water of the stream.

"I will go first," Ryu said, and stepped gingerly onto the first stone of the path in the water. He tested the sturdiness of it with his foot before continuing on to the next.

"It is safe," he declared and moved quickly to the other side of the stream.

Paulo followed next, with Brynn right behind him. Once they were all safely across, Paulo looked up in the sky. "I believe The Foothills are that way, on the other side of the trees," he said pointing straight ahead.

 Directly in front of them they could see a wide path through the dense forest, whose trees grew so close together that their trunks were almost touching. The children made their way toward it.

A little brown bird, like the one they had seen at the river, and the one that had helped Brynn at the large tree in the forest appeared at the entrance to the path. It hovered there for a moment, and the three children could clearly see it shake its head.

"I think it means to tell us that this is not the way," Brynn said, remembering how the little brown bird had showed her the invisible path to find Paulo and Ryu.

The bird nodded its head and chirped once. Moving a few lengths to the right of the path, the bird stopped in front of the trees and chirped three times.

"A bird such as this one showed me the way through the dense brush in the forest when I found you in the trunk of the tree. There was a path which was invisible. I could not see it, but it was there. I think there must be another such path through these trees," Brynn said, and moved to where the bird was hovering. "Just put your hands out in front of you, like this," Brynn said as she demonstrated, "And move slowly."

Ryu and Paulo watched as the little brown bird flew into the trees and seemed to vanish right before their eyes.

Seeing their fear, Brynn was quick to try and calm them, "Do not be afraid. Follow me." And with that she stretched her arms out in front of her, took a step forward, and disappeared into the trees just as the bird had.

A few moments later Brynn, or at least the top half of Brynn, poked back out of the trees. "Come on," she said with a wave and then disappeared again.

The boys paused, trying to understand what they had just seen. "We will go together," Ryu said to Paulo finally, knowing that the young boy must be somewhat frightened because he himself was.

The two boys stretched out their arms and walked slowly into the trees. They felt the same cool sensation Brynn had crossing through the vortex in the forest, and a moment later, they found themselves on the other side of the forest, in a clearing at the base of The Foothills.

The little brown bird, which had hovered on the other side waiting for the boys with Brynn, flew away then, back into the forest.

"See, I told you it would be alright," Brynn said smiling at her friends. And then turning to look at the mound of earth in the distance, covered in short brittle grass and as twice as high as the tallest tree in the forest, she urged, "Let us hurry. I know those hills, our village is just beyond."

The children began to run, with Ryu in the lead and Brynn keeping pace with Paulo once again. It was a few hundred lengths before the first hill when Ryu saw the large round stone buried into the dirt, its white face gleaming. It was another riddle. The three children were quiet as they read the words.

> *It is not what you see*
> *It is what you do not see*
> *It is the answer*

Brynn swallowed hard. She could feel her heart pounding in her chest. She had come to understand that The Riddles were warnings, warning of danger, and she felt panic creeping into the pit of her stomach. Ryu and Paulo felt it too.

Ryu struggled to push his fear aside. They were so close to the village now and he knew he must hold on to his courage, for his friends if not for himself.

"We will heed the warning should anything happen, but we must continue on. We only have a very short time now before we lose the light of the sun. We must hurry."

Brynn nodded in agreement and followed behind Ryu as he walked briskly toward the bottom of the hill. Paulo stared at the words of the riddle for a moment, and started to follow his friends. But right next to the rock, half hidden in the grass, a small light began to glow. Paulo stopped, and bending down he could see the smooth, multi colored face of a Legacy Stone.

"It must be a mistake," Paulo said to himself. "I am not a champion."

Still feeling guilty for deserting Brynn and for mistrusting Duvera, Paulo did not think he was worthy of this gift. Champions did not forsake their friends, did not err in judgment.

"This Legacy Stone does not belong to me," he thought. Picking up the stone, he held it for a moment, wondering if it had been meant for one of his friends.

Seeing that Brynn and Ryu were getting far ahead of him, Paulo slipped the Legacy Stone into the pouch tied to his belt and hurried to catch up.

Chapter 21

The hill was steep and rocky, and the three children had to crawl on their hands and knees in places in order to climb up. When he reached the top, Ryu waited a few moments for Paulo and Brynn join him. He could see the clearing below and the next hill they would have to climb, a few hundred lengths away. It was just as steep as this one. It was dusk now, and the sun was meeting the horizon. It would not be long until total darkness was upon them.

"We will have to slide down," Ryu said to his friends, and without hesitation, walked the few steps to the other side where the hill started to slope downward, turned and dropped to his stomach.

Using his feet to slow himself where it became too steep, Ryu quickly made his way to the bottom. Brynn and Paulo followed in the same manner, careful to avoid the rocks that jutted out from the hillside here and there.

Once safely down, Paulo, who was aching with thirst, opened the satchel Duvera had given him and drank from the flask of water. Both Ryu and Brynn also took a drink, grateful again to have met the kind old woman in the forest. Just as Brynn had finished and was replacing the cork back into the neck of the bottle, a voice called out from the top of the hill in front of them.

"Have you enough water in that flask for us?" a familiar voice asked.

The three children looked around, but could see no one. Laughter rang through the air, and the hairs on Brynn's arm began to prickle. She knew that laugh.

On top of the hill in front of them, the outline of what looked to be three children appeared. As the figures came into focus, what Ryu, Brynn and Paulo saw was truly unbelievable. The boy standing in the middle looked exactly like Ryu. The girl to his left was the spitting image of Brynn. And on the right, waving his hand to them like an old friend was an exact copy of Paulo.

"It is a trick!" Ryu said through clenched teeth. "They are spirits sent to trick us!"

"We are almost home," Paulo said in anguish as he looked at the visions before him, knowing that their village was just on the other side of the hill on which the apparitions stood.

"What are you?!" Brynn shouted to them, both scared and angry at the same time. She knew these were false spirits, as L'Har had been. She would not let them deceive her or her friends. She stood tall, preparing to face whatever tricks they had in store.

The visions seemed to float down the hill then, stopping only a dozen lengths away from the children. Paulo, Brynn and Ryu could only watch motionless, fear taking a firm hold on them. With each of their twins standing directly in front of them, Ryu, Brynn and Paulo felt as though they were looking into a mirror. The features, hair, clothing even the expressions that the spirits wore were identical to their own.

"What are you?" Brynn asked again, breathlessly as she studied the creature before her. The scar above her eye where she had fallen as a young child and banged her head on a pile of fire wood, just learning to walk, was there. The freckles that scattered across her noise, each was in the exact same place. She could even see scrapes on the palms of this spirit's hands, exactly the same as those she had gotten from tripping over the tree root at the very beginning of The Crossing.

"We are you, Brynn," her look- alike answered, with a mischievous smile.

"No you are not!" Paulo said bravely, finding his strength after all. He would not let himself be fooled again as he had been with L'Har. And as he remembered Duvera's warning: *the three of you are much stronger together than you could ever be alone*, he reached out and took Brynn's hand in his.

Brynn understood and reached out to hold Ryu's hand in her other one.

The vision in front of Paulo smiled warmly. "Oh, but I am you Paulo," it said sweetly. "I have four brothers and sisters; Pia, Piero, Patia and Pirtia. My father is head of The Sciences Council, I like to climb up to the top of the tallest trees in the village and when I am grown, I want to be a hunter."

Paulo felt frozen where he stood. How did this spirit know these things?

"My name is Brynn," said the spirit whose long red hair and green eyes were an exact duplicate of the real

Brynn. "I miss my father, I would like to stop growing soon so that I will not always be the tallest girl in my lesson class, and I wish my mother were stronger so I would not have to take care of her, and she would take care of me."

Brynn felt tears welling up in her eyes. How did this spirit know her deepest feelings?

"And I am Ryu," Ryu's twin said matter-of-factly. "My mother is a village elder, I want to be just like my brother Roque when I am older and I have secretly had love in my heart for Brynn since we were six years old."

Ryu's cheeks flushed with a mixture of fury and embarrassment. Brynn squeezed his hand tighter, and managed a soft smile.

Paulo, however, was quick to defend his friends. "What do you want?" he spat.

"We have followed you as the path took you through the briar tunnel and into the caves," his twin answered.

"We watched as you struggled in the river, ate by the well and were foolishly trapped in the big old tree. We watched as you rested in the cottage in the forest and ran by the stream. We watched as you found each of The Riddles and did not heed their warnings."

"We have watched you all through your journey," the vision of Ryu said. "We have watched as each of you failed."

"Failed?" Brynn asked, incredulously, "How have we failed? We are almost home."

"It was your pride and stubbornness that caused your fall into the river," her twin answered her unkindly.

"You were trying to be a hero, just as Roque had been, when you left your friends to save others," Ryu's copy said to him sarcastically.

"And you Paulo," the spirit that stood in front of him said with distain, "you thought of no one but yourself when you followed L'Har into the forest."

"Each of you has failed," the spirit of Ryu said angrily.

"We did not fail," Ryu insisted, equally as angry. "We have made mistakes, yes," he continued, "but we have not failed."

"To forsake a friend is to fail," The spirit of Paulo said harshly. "And for that, there is a price."

"A price?" Brynn asked, timidly, "What price must we pay for our mistakes other than that which we have already paid?"

"In order to set things right, one of you must stay here with us on the paths of The Crossing," answered Paulo's spirit twin.

"Stay with you? What do you mean?" Paulo asked, panic gripping his heart.

Ryu's twin looked at him sharply, and his words were dripping with distain . "It has been decided, only two of you shall continue on. It has been decided that one of you shall have to die."

Chapter 22

"Die?" Ryu spoke the word as though he had never used it before, almost as though he did not understand its meaning. "Why must one of us die?"

"I have already told you," his spirit twin answered, annoyed, "it is the price that is required for the mistakes that have been made."

"By all rights, you should have died in the river," her twin stated looking at Brynn with a scowl. "And Ryu and Paulo," she said sneering at the two of them, "you both should have perished in the trunk of the old tree."

"But we did not," Paulo stated, "Brynn saved us."

"And Ryu and Paulo saved me from the river," Brynn said angrily.

"You had help!" Brynn's twin growled to them. "The Somethings helped you. Without their help, you would be dead!"

"But many others before us made mistakes and were helped along the path of The Crossing," Paulo said, recalling many stories he had been told by his father. "Why must one of us die?"

"No one helped us!" Brynn's spirit twin said through clenched teeth, her eyes full of rage. "No one!"

"It does not matter!" Ryu's twin shouted, his face contorted with anger. "We shall take one of you, as was meant to be!"

"Run," Brynn said to her friends urgently as she started to step forward. "They cannot stop us."

The vision that was her twin waved her hand then, and a wall of fire appeared just in front of the three children. Its flames were half a dozen lengths high, and so red hot they threatened to sear their clothing. They hurried a few steps back in order to escape the heat.

"You can not run," Paulo's twin shouted over the sound of the raging flames.

He glared at them through the fire for a few moments before waving his hand downward, and as he did, the fire extinguished itself as quickly as it appeared. "You cannot run from this," he continued, "One of you will indeed die."

"But as a courtesy," Brynn's twin said sarcastically, "we will allow you to choose. We will allow you to choose which one of you will die."

"So which will it be?" Ryu's twin asked, impatiently. "Will it be you Ryu?" he asked, looking to the boy who had been the leader for much of the journey.

"If indeed you mean to keep one of us and end our life right here and now, then yes, I choose myself," Ryu said bravely.

"No, Ryu!" Brynn said, her words full of pain. Ryu let go of her hand, and Paulo's, and stepped forward.

"I choose myself because it is The Right Thing," Ryu said. He looked at Brynn then, tears brimming in his eyes. "I have always held you close in my heart Brynn, and I cannot bear the thought of you never returning home to your mother. She needs you to be strong for her, and you are. You are strong and smart. Someday, I know you will lead our village as one of The Elders. It cannot be you who dies."

He looked to Paulo then. "And you my friend," he said smiling warmly, "your mind is sharp, and your heart is true. I know some day you will be a hunter, as you dream of being. Or maybe you will be head of The Sciences Council as your father is."

Ryu reached out to ruffle Paulo's hair with his hand. "Whatever it is you choose, I know you will succeed. You will be a great man."

"So it is decided then?" Brynn's spirit twin said, moving forward toward Ryu.

"No!" Brynn shouted stepping between him and the apparition. The spirit stopped and moved back in line beside the other two. She turned to look at Ryu. "I can not let you die!" Turning to look at the three spirits she exclaimed, "It should be me, take me!"

"You wish to die?" Paulo's twin asked her pointedly.

"Yes," Brynn said hurriedly, "I mean, no, I do not wish to die. But if the choice is Ryu or myself, I choose myself."

She turned to look into Ryu's eyes. "I too have always held you close in my heart Ryu, but I have been a selfish friend. There have been many times when I have acted recklessly, without a moments thought to the danger I may have placed you in. And I do love my mother, very much, but I think it is because of all I do that she is caught in her grief and unable to move forward." She turned again to face the three spirits before them. "It should be me who dies."

"And what about you Paulo?" his spirit twin asked with a wicked grin. "Will you not offer yourself up to be taken? You have many brothers and sisters, and should you die, one of them would surely take your place within the family." And then with a laugh he said, "In a house full of children, you would hardly be missed."

"It is true," Paulo answered, "I do not hold a place of importance in my family or in my village. And if you truly mean to keep one of us here with you, then I will volunteer myself." He took a step forward, but as his gaze fell upon each of the dark spirits before him, he suddenly recognized the truth. "But you do not mean to let us choose do you?" he asked. "You have already decided which one of us will die. This is a game to you."

The three spirits laughed wickedly. It was Ryu's copy which finally spoke. "Yes, Paulo, you are right. It was decided before. But what fun would it be to just tell you straight away? We have so enjoyed hearing you plead for each other's lives."

The spirits started to float slowly towards Brynn, Paulo and Ryu then, fury and hatred in their eyes.

The Legacy Stone in Paulo's pouch began to glow with an intense white light.

"A Legacy Stone!" Ryu cried in desperation.

Terrified, Brynn hoped its power could help save them now.

The words of the last riddle came rushing into Paulo's mind.

It is not what you see
It is what you do not see
It is the answer

Quickly, Paulo studied each of the spirits. In an instant, he knew the answer. Reaching into his pouch, he hurriedly withdrew The Legacy Stone. With all of his might he threw it directly at Ryu's spirit twin. The stone hit the spirit in the stomach, directly above the rope belt tied there. The three spirits seemed frozen in the air.

A bright white ball of light opened, and a swirling vortex appeared. Each spirit's eyes were wide in disbelief as they were sucked into the vortex one by one, then the light seemed to fold into itself and was gone.

The children stared at the empty space for a moment, but then rushed into each other's arms. Holding each other tightly, the tears flowed freely as they wept.

Chapter 23

"How did you know?" Ryu asked Paulo as the three finally let go of one another. "How did you know what to do?"

Brushing away the tears from his face, Paulo swallowed hard before answering. "The last riddle," he said, "It is not what you see, but what you do not see. When The Legacy Stone began to glow, those words came to me. When I looked at the spirits I knew what was missing."

"Missing?" Brynn asked as she struggled to compose herself.

"Yes, Brynn, what was not there," Paulo answered quickly. "The spirits were an exact copy of each of us. They had the same hair, eyes, voices, even the same clothing. Only something was missing." He reached out to touch the stripe of color sewn to the arm of Ryu's tunic. "Their clothing was the same, except for this. Ryu's spirit twin did not have a red arm band."

"You saved us," Ryu said reaching to embrace his friend one more. He gave Paulo a warm smile. "Thank you Paulo, thank you."

"Yes, Paulo you saved us all," Brynn said gratefully, but then was confused. "Why did you not tell us you had found a Legacy Stone?"

Paulo's cheeks blushed red as he stepped away from Ryu. "When I found it by the rock of the last riddle, I thought it was a mistake," he said shyly. "I thought it had been meant for one of you."

129

Ryu gave a small laugh, "Well my friend, you were wrong. The Legacy Stone showed what Brynn and I already knew. You are very smart and very brave. You are a true Champion!" Paulo could not help but grin at Ryu's kind words.

Up in the sky, the crescent shaped moon shone brightly, and darkness was only a few moments away. Brynn looked to the hill in front of them. "Come on," she said as she started towards it, "It is time to go home." Ryu and Paulo followed. They ran the last few hundred lengths of the clearing together.

Climbing the last hill proved to be no small task, and the children had to scale it on their hands and knees. Its face was mostly broken rock, and if not careful, one could easily slide right back down to the bottom.

Once they had reached the top the three stood together, and they could see the torches that had been lit on the other side of the clearing below. They knew only their families would be waiting for them there in the Great Hall, as was customary at the end of each Crossing. There would food and drink, and warm baths drawn for them back at their cottages.

First thing tomorrow morning, the children were expected to meet with the village Elders and recount the events of their journey so that they could be recorded in The Book. In the afternoon the whole village would join them in a celebration, with music, and dancing and a great feast of roasted meats and fancy cakes.

Night was fully upon them now as Ryu, Paulo and Brynn slid carefully the down the steep slope on the other side of the Foothill, with Ryu going first. He thought of Roque as he maneuvered around the many rocks, knowing that his brother would be proud that he had found a Legacy Stone, that he too was a Champion. But he did not feel like a Champion. He knew it would be a long while before he went searching for adventure again, if ever. At that moment, all Ryu felt was an intense longing to be back home with his mother and father and the comfort and safety of his home.

Brynn was also longing to be back with her mother then. Now, she welcomed the routine, the calm of her every day life. Imagining her mother's smiling face, she knew that she would never again take her for granted. Although she missed her father immensely, Brynn knew from then on that the love that she shared with her mother would be more than enough for her.

Paulo's thoughts were of Ryu and Brynn as he travelled down the slope. He knew the bond of friendship that was crafted by all they had been through on their journey could never be broken. He knew that once back in their village, their lives would be intertwined from that day forward. They had overcome many obstacles, faced great evil and together they had found their way home. All three were Champions.

At the bottom of the hill, the children were immersed in their own thoughts as they walked the through the clearing together. Only a few hundred lengths away from the light of the torches, Paulo came to an abrupt stop. Ryu and Brynn stopped as well, and turned to look at their friend. His expression was solemn.

"We cannot tell them," Paulo spoke quietly. "We cannot tell them about L'Har."

"Paulo," Brynn said as she squeezed his hand gently, "You need not be ashamed. L'Har was an evil spirit who tricked us all. The Elders, our parents, they will understand this."

"No Brynn", he answered, his mind filled with visions of all that had happened, "Not our parents, or the Elders, it is the other children we cannot tell about L'Har. We can not tell our friends and the others in our lesson groups the story of L'Har, or about the spirits on the hill. I cannot even tell my brothers and sisters."

"What do you mean?" Ryu asked, confused.

"When my father would tell me stories of The Crossing," Paulo explained, "he would talk of The Somethings and The Nothings which presented themselves to children on the path in many different forms – a song in the wind, a pattern of leaves..."

"Or a school of helpful fish," Ryu said with a smile.

"Yes," Paulo continued, managing a small smile himself, "or a school of helpful fish." All the children in our village hear stories of The Something and the Nothings," he grew serious once again, "But every time my father would tell me those stories, there always seemed to be something he was not telling me, things he would deliberately leave out."

"Yes," Brynn agreed, "my mother and father, when he was alive, also seemed to be holding something back when they would tell stories of The Crossing."

"It is so we would not be afraid," Paulo said with certainty. "They do not tell us about the spirits because they know that we would be too frightened to walk the path of The Crossing."

Glancing back to where they had come from, his eyes were filled with a knowing look, "No child would ever want to take the journey of The Crossing if they knew of the evil that is waiting to harm them."

The torches by The Great Hall seemed to shine much brighter in the darkness now. With an even greater sense of urgency than before, the three friends held on to each other's hands and began to run towards the light.

http://mommywhatis.com

www.ingramcontent.com/pod-product-compliance
Lightning Source LLC
Chambersburg PA
CBHW020249150626
46552CB00020B/727